PULSE

When Gravity Fails

Pulse

By

John Freitas

ISBN-13: 9781530117567

Acknowledgment

Thank you NASA for everything you do.

"A fish swimming in the ocean does not know it is in the water until a wave comes."
Dr. Paulo Restrepo - Marlo-Pitts Observatory

The one o'clock sun shone bright in the clear blue skies of Southeast Texas. Christine was in the laundry room, transferring clothes from the washing machine to a laundry basket. The warm and dry weather in rural Brenham made it perfect to hang a large white sheet and clothes on a clothesline. The thirty four year old mother, with blue eyes and freckles peppered on her face gathered several clothespins, picked up the heavy basket and walked to an open door leading to inside of the house. An eight year old boy and a six year old girl were playing in the living room.

"Kids, today is a beautiful day, why don't you go outside to play?"

"Ok mom, as soon as I finish this game." answers the boy. The girl is too busy brushing and talking to a doll.

The mother opened the laundry room door to the outside, the central alarm beeped a few times and a breeze of warm air entered the room. It was a little windy outside. The kids bikes were leaning against the house, not too far from the vegetable garden that was now populated with tomatoes, peppers and a few okra plants.

Christine walked up to the clothes line, puts the basket down and hung the first garment. They have been living in the country side for 6 months now. After being laid off from an oil company in downtown Houston, her husband found a management position in an ice cream factory nearby. Because the cost of real estate is low in this part of the state, they bought a three acre land with a two story house in a place that seemed to be in the middle of nowhere. There were no other houses around them.

The land was surrounded by a cattle farm meadow in one side and a corn field in another, so the three acres sometimes felt like one thousand. Christine liked the life in the country most of the time. She felt calmer with the constant contact with the outdoors which brought the fragrance of her lavender flowers, the dance of the butterflies and the singing birds. The air felt cleaner than in the city, but she missed the busy neighborhood a little. She especially missed the quick access to supermarkets and stores.

The family's two German Shepherds came to check on her with a wagging tail and a smiling face. They are two months old. The female licked her leg while the male grabbed the shoe laces on her tennis shoe and pulled it. Christine looked down and smiled.

"Hey, leave my shoe alone!" shouted out Christine while shaking her foot. The dogs hopped around her with their tongues out for a few more seconds and left.

Christine held a clothespin between her teeth and picked up a large white sheet. She threw one side across the line and started spreading it. The sheet shone bright against the sun making difficult to look straight at it. The wind gently pushed the sheet against her face.

"Mom, come here quick!" called the boy from inside the house.

"Mom!" called the girl.

"What happened?" shouted the mother while running towards the house still holding a clothespin.

As Christine approached the door, she felt light headed. She ran through the laundry room with the sensation she was going to lose her balance at any minute and she had a tickling feeling in her stomach. It felt as she was walking in an aisle of a descending airplane.

Christine stopped at the living room entrance. She let go the clothespin and used both hands to grab each side of the door frame. She looked at the children and gasped.

"Look Mom, we can fly!" said her son in an excited voice, while bouncing from a wall towards the ceiling. All the toys were hovering a foot above the ground, lightly colliding against each other. Her daughter was slowly coming down from the ceiling towards the sofa and as soon her feet touched it, she jumped up and back towards the ceiling, giggling.

The clothespin was still falling in slow motion half way from the floor, while spinning on its axis.

***

Sean Grayson and Carter Strove -- West Memphis, Arkansas

The alarm blared and instructions crackled through the speakers. Sean Grayson was used to the interruptions, but it startled him anyway. He gave the Stroganoff one more stir and then tossed the wooden spoon aside on the counter where it left an oily, brown smear of grease.

He shut off the heat to the stove burner he was using and pushed the pan back onto one of the cold eyes. Sean double checked the dials on the stove again out of reflex to be sure they were off. There had been more than one company that had run out of the firehouse to go put out someone else's stove fire only to come back and find their own quarters full of black smoke. No West Memphis firefighters had burned down their houses yet, but the town was small and the stories always made the paper.

"Let's go, Grayson," Lieutenant Foster shouted.

Sean turned away from the stove and ran to gear up. "Just double checking the burners, L. T."

"Didn't ask. Don't care. Don't make me ask twice, Firefighter."

"Yes, sir."

"Beef Stroganoff is a stupid breakfast anyway."

Sean chuckled. "Yes, sir."

He gritted his teeth as he ran down the stairs. There was the traditional pole, but the stairs were closer to the kitchen. Since Lt. Jim Foster had replaced Brosky, he was still flexing his muscles and establishing his authority. Foster had been a firefighter across the Mississippi River in Memphis, Tennessee. There was animosity about him promoting up from the outside and especially from Tennessee. Sean tried to stay out of his sights.

Most of the messages calling the order to load up were automated and used a soothing woman's voice. Carter Strove's brother Michael was in the Air Force and said they used the same voice for the messages on the helicopters and fighters. Some study had shown that men attuned to a woman's voice more than a man's. As Sean thought about his ex, he wondered, if that could be true. *Maybe you just couldn't tune her out*, he thought. Thinking about this brought up his anger floating to the surface against Carter. Sean pushed it back down in his mind.

He had missed the details about the call and location on the fire as his mind swirled around his most recent regrets in a life full of them.

"See?" Sean said to no one. "I didn't tune into anything she said."

He hit the locker room and pulled on his protective suiting as the other guys finished off.

"Running behind," Carter said.

The other guys looked between the two men as they dashed out to the truck. Sean knew they were expecting a dust-up. Everyone had been waiting for the fight and it might still come, but Sean wouldn't do it on a call and he was low on energy from not getting a taste of his Stroganoff.

"Yeah." Sean left it at that and Carter walked past Sean with his head down. He was adjusting the strap to his mask.

Sean rushed through the rest and ran after Carter. When Carter Strove had first joined up with the company, there had been a firefighter named Horrace Carter that was old as dirt and tough as nails. Everyone called him Carter or Old Carter. Carter Strove then became Black Carter. Old Carter retired, but Strove was still Black Carter. No one thought anything of it until Lt. Foster took over after Brosky. Foster put a stop to the nickname. Memphis had a storied racial history and Foster wasn't interested in tempting trouble. So, Black Carter went to just being Carter or sometimes "Just Carter" when the guys were feeling hot about the new Lieutenant's rules.

Sean hit the truck last as it was already moving. He leapt through the open door behind the driver and slammed it closed. As he dropped his kit and took the empty seat, he saw he was right next to "Just Carter."

Carter licked his lips and looked away through one of the back windows. Sean wondered if the guys had arranged it so they would be forced to sit by each other. He didn't think they would.

Carter spoke over the sound of the siren. "Found your little present in my locker this morning."

"Don't know what you are talking about," Sean said as he found buckles to check on his coat.

"Okay," Carter said. "It was impressive though. I didn't know you could stretch a condom all the way across the top of a helmet like that."

"Maybe you just have never had to roll them down that far before," Sean said.

"You can ask …" Carter stopped talking. Sean had an idea of how Carter planned to finish that sentence. It was good that he stopped. Sean wouldn't have lashed out – not then, but the other guys were watching the exchange. It was good that he stopped. Sean realized through his bubbling anger that Carter had done it out of basic respect for their friendship and not out of any fear. Sean knew Carter well enough to know it took more than that to scare him. Carter shifted to another sentence. "Maybe we can compare helmets when we get back from the fire since you are so interested in mine. I take your message though, brother. Condom over the helmet over my head? Not very subtle."

"I didn't do it, Carter. You should report it to the L. T. since he told everyone to stop hurting your feelings about all this."

"Yeah, right." Carter shook his head. "Then I can get a canary hung in my locker by a string, huh?"

"If the Foster doesn't want us calling you Black Carter, I'm guessing he'd probably hit the ceiling if we strung up a bird in your locker."

Carter actually laughed out loud. Sean felt a sting in the back of his throat and behind his eyes. He didn't realize in that moment how much he had missed his friend's laugh. He missed it more than he missed his wife.

"You two were already divorced when I started seeing her," Carter said. Any goodwill that was building from the laugh was blasted away by that statement. "I swear it."

"It doesn't matter, Carter. There's a code and there's a line and you crossed it. Every bit of bad blood you've dealt with has come from that. We fight for each other. We don't take up with each other's wives – divorced or not. Don't act like you don't get that. She's the mother of my boys and you're running around playing step daddy to them."

"You knew she would date someone someday."

"Don't act like you don't get it, Carter. We are friends. You should know better."

Sean had almost said they *were* friends instead of they are friends. It would have been a very different statement and the moment scared him a little. They were about to go into a burning building together. This was a dangerous conversation to be having right now.

"I do get it, Sean, but I love her. I'm sorry that's true, but it is. I don't get close to people like that often. I've never felt this way about anyone I've dated. I can't just throw that away. I can't do it even though it is the right thing to do. I'm sorry, brother."

Sean turned his head away and chewed at the inside of his mouth. "Stop talking to me right now, Carter."

One of the guys across from them said, "Yes, please, shut up, both of you. It's like a soap opera I can't ever turn off."

Sean felt the empty feeling inside again. It was like his guts were inflated with helium and he was about to float right up out of his life. He had felt it when Tabitha had confronted him about being addicted to Oxycodone after he hurt his back. He had kept working and kept taking it even when he had to buy it illegally from tweekers north of town. She had told him to quit or she was leaving with the boys. He hadn't and she did.

He felt it again when he took a leave of absence for "medical reasons" and checked into rehab. Carter knew and even with all the garbage they put him through when the guys found out he was dating Tabby, he hadn't said anything to anyone.

Sean suspected some of the other guys knew too. It was a small town. He suspected some of them were watching him and Carter because they wanted to see if it would push him back onto the Oxy. They would continue to work with a guy screwing someone else's wife. They wouldn't risk their lives on a guy that was high or unstable because he just wanted to be high.

Sean pushed the empty, floating feeling back down and cleared his mind.

The truck stopped and they unloaded. The apartment building was engulfed on one side. Two other companies from the battalion were already there. One was dousing the side of the burn. The other was taking people down from windows.

The Captain shouted orders to Lt. Foster that Sean couldn't hear. He watched the flames lick out of windows blackening the brick. He turned to help the crew hook up another hose. The entire building would be up soon. This was about to become a surround and drown situation.

6

Foster called, "Carter, Baker, Grayson, we need one more team to pull survivors from the interior rooms. Lt. Timms will assign you a path at the door. Move."

The three ran toward the building as the others were hooking up the hose. Sean pulled on his mask as the Lieutenant at the door showed them where to go up. "You got ten minutes tops, boys. Any longer and the place will fall in around you and anyone we leave up there. Watch each other."

Sean stepped in first without thinking about it. Baker grabbed his belt and Carter grabbed Baker behind him. Sean engaged his oxygen as they took the stairs. After three steps they were surrounded by blinding smoke. The fire and water were concentrated on the other side of the building, but the stairs already felt wet and spongy under his feet. Sean suspected that they had less than ten minutes.

Sean shouted through his mask. "Anyone here? We are here to help. Hello? Are you here?"

In this level of smoke, he suspected that anyone alive would be unconscious and quickly moving to not alive.

Baker used the head of his ax to strike just above the doorknob once and twice before the door flung open. Smoke hung thin around the ceiling inside, but much thinner than out in the halls and stairs.

Thicker, black smoke poured into the unit from the open doorway. The trio followed to walls and opened bedrooms as they shouted. Breakfast plates and a half full glass of milk sat on the table. The glass had balloons on it and reminded Sean of the ones Holden and Grant drank from back when they were a complete family. Holden was eight and moving away from those types of cups. Grant was recently four and was only just pushing into using a big boy cup.

The men looked under beds and in closets where kids tended to hide. Sean kicked open the bathroom and saw the plastic shower curtain with balloons printed on it. The words on the balloons read "Up, Up, and AWAY!!!" The toothbrush was a superhero that Sean didn't know. He had a blue cape and was in mid flight.

"Hello?" There was no answer and they moved back out into the hall.

Three steps up and Sean kicked someone in the leg. A woman in a waitress's uniform lay passed out on the steps. Sean leaned down and saw her nametag read Cathy. There was a red balloon sticker on it with the word "Up!" She was breathing. Sean shook her, but she didn't open her eyes. "She's alive, but not responding."

"I'll take her," Carter said. "Try to search one more floor before they pull us."

Carter grabbed her up in his arms and ran down the stairs without waiting for an answer. Baker and Sean hit two more apartments. On their way out of the last empty one, a wash of dark water poured off the landing above onto the stairs. Flame belched over the edge above them and the boards snapped above their heads showing thick darkness beyond.

"We need to hurry." Sean took a step.

Baker pulled Sean back by his arm. "No. Wait."

The landing above crackled and collapsed into the stairs. The stairs broke through and dumped into an electrical room under them. Flame flashed up from the room below. The fire had come in around them.

"Pull out! All teams, out now. Over." The order came over the radio at Sean's shoulder.

Baker pulled again and Sean followed him down the stairs cluttered with smoldering, wet debris.

The radio crackled again. "Sean? This is Black Carter. There is a boy, seven years old, in that first apartment we searched. Mother says he's in there. We missed him. Over."

Lt. Foster's voice broke over. "Don't use that nickname, for God's sake, and the pull out order was given. The building is coming down."

Sean stopped on the stairs and Baker turned and looked up at him. "We are out of time. We searched. He may have already been pulled out. What'd you want to do, Sean?"

Sean thought about the balloon sticker on the waitress's nametag, the cup and the shower curtain. He hadn't pulled back the shower curtain.

Sean turned and ran back up the stairs.

2

Captain Michael Strove – Pacific Ocean off the coast of Russia

Captain Michael Strove banked and put a little more distance between his wing and the imaginary wall of air that represented Russian waters. He was well within International water, but the three Russian megs racing into his radar from the south told him that they did not fully trust his judgment. These cat and mouse games were common practice, but since the collision over the Black Sea on the other side of the continent, these games were more tense.

Michael thought he could understand their point. If a Russian fighter came fifteen miles off the coast of America, they would have an even stronger reaction. It wasn't Michael's place to decide whether his missions were the best decision. He was just to carry them out successfully.

The bogies were closing the distance behind him and spreading out their formation. They weren't locking weapons yet, so that was good. When he was a kid, he and his older brother Carter had played fighter pilots. They always imagined seeing the enemy and watching the bullets ring off of metal. The reality was that dog fights occurred too far away to see each other with the naked eye usually. If it turned violent, missiles would close the distance and make the red and green dots disappear from the screen.

He supposed if they collided over the Black Sea, that was a different story.

Michael decided he had stirred enough trouble and put on speed toward the north. The Russians increased speed as he expected.

He saw the pulsing colors of the northern lights twisting in the darkness of the sky ahead. The water was shockingly blue as it curved over the horizon toward the Bering Strait.

He was on radio silence until he was back within American territory on his way back to the base in Alaska. He thought it probably didn't matter if the enemy already had him, but they were orders and it wasn't his place to disobey them.

He prepared to bank again, but then lights became blindingly bright before vanishing. He blinked and stared forward for a moment longer.

Then the lights returned, but ran through the range of colors in a rapid pattern. It didn't look real. They twisted into circles like they were following some current then into a flowing knot that reminded him of the infinity symbol.

The view twisted and the ocean turned from the familiar curve of the Earth from this altitude to a tunnel where the water appeared to loop around onto itself. The northern lights burned in the center. Michael got the sensation that the plane was corkscrewing and that's what created the distortion.

When he looked down at the instruments, he realized he was flying right. Though his senses told him to pull out of the spin, his training told him to trust the instruments. The reason rich doctors and the sons of important politicians crashed their private planes was because they wanted to believe their eyes and feelings. They would get lost in storms and come out flying upside down refusing to trust that they were wrong and the instruments were right.

Captain Stove prepared to bank out over the ocean to see if the Russians would break off on open water before they intercepted. Then, the instruments winked out.

"Now I'm in trouble." He heard his voice over the speakers in his own helmet.

They sputtered back on, but rattled through data with the same confusion he was seeing outside. *Now there is no one to trust*, he thought.

The engine tone changed and the metal screamed around him as he felt the G forces increase like he was in a hard roll. The intermittent images on the screen still told him he was flying right, but he felt the blood leaving his head and he wanted to toggle out of a spin he wasn't actually in.

The canopy cracked and the white lines of fracture spider webbed out above him. The material was a polymer plastic and could be destroyed a dozen different ways, but cracking like glass was not one of them.

The automated female voice began rattling off a damage report. The data scrolled over the screen faster than she could nag it into his ears in her soothing tone.

Despite the force pressing down on him, he forced his head and shoulders up to look across the craft in a visual check. The smart

10

materials of the fighter were morphing with a pressure that he had to now believe was real. On the ground, the seams across the wings were open and even leaked, but in flight, the bird was solid and flexible. As the wings bowed under the forces outside, the seams were opening again in flight.

He felt the response of the plane change. In the midst of her running damage report, Michael heard that he was losing altitude.

He was over cold water. If he ejected, which could be fatal at these speeds anyway, he would land in the frigid ocean. He could freeze to death or best case, be rescued by the Russians. He could fly in and eject over land, but after the Black Sea incident, that would create enormous problems – maybe even an international incident.

More importantly, Captain Strove's fighter had proprietary technology. The Russians recovering his wreckage would be worse than the Pakistani army discovering the stealth helicopter after the mission against Bin Laden's compound.

He knew he had to put the craft down in the water. It wasn't good enough to eject and let it crash for the Russians to fish out. He had to spear it in hard enough to break it up and put the pieces on the bottom. That would give his people time to secure the site and prevent the Russians from mounting a recovery. One airman dead would be a letter home, but no international crisis.

Captain Michael Strove decided to take the craft as far out into the ocean toward U.S. waters before he crashed to make it as easy for his side and as hard for theirs as he could. It wouldn't be far though. He was losing altitude fast and the plane was acting like it was carrying three times its weight.

Michael thought about Carter. Their father had died of a heart attack years ago. Their mother was in a nursing home and didn't remember much most of the time. Carter would go to tell her after he got the letter, but she wouldn't even remember him or Michael. Carter was going to carry the burden of this all alone. This would be a crisis of one.

The weight lifted off the wings and the plane rocketed upward in response to the force that Michael was still trying to fight, but was suddenly gone. The view outside popped back to normal and the plane tumbled as it soared upward.

The instruments stopped flickering, but the damage report still lilted in a woman's soothing tones inside his helmet. Michael fought the spin and righted the plane only to find he was flying over Russian waters.

He banked hard to loop back on course. "You lied to me."

The computer still soothingly listed everything that was broken despite his accusation.

He caught sight of the three bogies on radar. They were flying wild. One was looping hard over land, another was zig zagging out to sea, and the third vanished off of the radar not far behind Michael which meant either blown up or down.

Michael decided to see if he could crash in Alaska just for the hell of it. He wanted to get away as fast as possible in case the Russian nearest him had dropped under radar for an attack.

The G forces settled onto him again harder than before and he cursed. The instruments flashed on and off. The smart materials bowed and the controls locked.

Michael tried to fight to break it free, but he raced forward and off course.

He saw he was over land now and it had to be Russia. He cursed again and then he started to pray.

Black spots filled his vision from the edges like insects crawling over and covering the controls in front of him. He heard his own, harsh breathing in his ears through the speakers. His fingers went numb and he wasn't sure if he was holding the controls anymore.

Before he blacked out, Michael saw the land below him become water again even though he had not changed course as the fighter undulated on the wind with its locked controls. Some part of his hazy mind knew that was important, but he couldn't think clearly enough to make out why.

Michael whispered. "Sorry, Carter."

3

Roman Nikitin – Taiga forest region, eastern Russia, ranger outpost
327

Roman Nikitin weaved between the trees on his way up the slope.
The ground went from the spongy feel of moss, leaf bed, and high
water table to the rockier surface of the hill. He saw the observation
tower near the top in a break between the conifers that clung to this hill.
He had to navigate by sight points as there was no proper trail even
after all these months of patrolling the same area.

The loggers were almost close enough to see from the towers now.
He could sometimes spot the smoke plumes from their work. Soon they
would be cutting bare patches through the landscape. Half of Roman
felt bad about nature being scarred for progress this deep in the
wilderness. The other half of him hoped they cut down every tree in
Russia as he was here on partial exile for being born into the wrong
family that made enemies with the wrong family.

He reached high enough that he could see the river to the north. It
was not an important river to most people and did not even appear on
most maps. It was important to Roman because it marked the southern
border of a military camp. If he wandered across, he would likely be
shot. Part of his job as an exiled ranger was to stop explorers and
loggers from accidentally crossing into the dead zone. There had never
been explorers and the loggers had not yet come nearly this far.

The crackling noise echoed through the dense forest behind him.
Roman turned and looked back through the trees. He was still not high
enough to spot what the cause was. He had played it off to loggers
being closer than he thought the first time. He decided it was just rotten
trees falling the second time. But now he was running out of logical
answers.

His mother had believed there were spirits in the wilderness of
Russia – that the empire had earned many ghosts. She considered
herself Russian, but had strong reasons to distrust the motherland.
Roman's father spent most of his life trying to keep her quiet about her
concerns, spiritual or otherwise, around other people. If she were still
alive, she would blame herself for Roman's exile.

Roman pictured tigers. He had been assured a dozen times that there were no tigers in this part of Russia, but his superiors had lied to him often. The radio and electricity in the abandoned listening post that served as his ranger station and cabin did not work. They were also not easy to repair, if broken. Supplies did not come regularly and Roman was surviving by spending much of his days hunting animals for food instead of protecting them from illegal hunting.

"Tigers climb trees, but they wouldn't be knocking them down," Roman whispered to himself in Russian. "Unless they were very large tigers."

He turned and continued his journey up the hill.

Roman reached the iron ladder and felt the rust grind off under his hands as he climbed. On a few of the steps, he felt the ladder waver on its connecting bolts. On a few other steps, he felt the entire tower shift with his weight and a light wind.

He reached the belly of the observation deck and pushed against the underside of the trapdoor. It was jammed shut from wear, rust, and the constant shifting of the poorly maintained tower. He pounded up on it until his wrist hurt.

Roman spouted out every Russian curse he knew twice plus a few Yiddish ones he had heard from his mother at night when she argued with his father. Roman twisted around on the ladder so that his boot was above him against the hatch. The entire ladder rocked hard to one side with the off balance stance. He fully expected to have the rungs snap under him and he would fall bodily into the jaws of a giant tiger sneaking through the trees below.

He bent his knee and kicked once, then twice. The door gave slightly. He drew back and kicked again feeling pain lace up through his joints. "Why do I go on with these empty comings and goings? I kick against the goads like a stupid donkey."

He kicked again and the hatch burst open with a crash.

Roman righted himself and climbed up onto the deck. Safety regulations called for closing the hatch back, but Roman pictured himself dying of starvation trapped above the Russian wilderness. He determined to just not stumble through the opening and fall to his death.

He spoke a phrase in English he had learned from TV shows on the Internet before he was assigned a post with no electricity. "Note to self."

Roman raised the binoculars to scan over the top of the forest looking for lost hunters, loggers, or evidence of giant tigers. He saw none.

The sound of another crack and crash rolled up past his ears in the tower. He leaned his elbows on the wood shelf of the open observation bay and scanned again.

He still didn't see it, but kept his eyes to the lenses and the glasses aimed out toward the west below him. He mumbled in English. "Tyger, Tyger, burning bright …"

Roman knew the story of the meteorite striking in the middle of Siberia and flattening miles of forest in an instant. It had happened in the early part of the twentieth century, but like most stories in Russia, it was told as if it happened yesterday. The impact had been so great that it was like an atomic blast before the Americans ever invented and dropped the first bomb. Like most stories it Russia, some told it as something beyond natural – the invasion of some dark force from beyond this world.

Roman was farther south and east than the tundra of Siberia in the temperate forests of the Taiga. Also, if an atomic sized meteorite strike happened, he would not have time to wonder what it was. But maybe a shower of smaller rocks could strike. They might cause a fire that he had no chance of outrunning or one might punch right through his skull. *No one would even notice I was gone*, he thought.

"Taiga, Taiga, burning bright … Note to self: Do not get killed by falling space rock."

He saw the tree go down and then the sound hit his ear a fraction of a second later. He looked for motion or a cause from the ground, but saw none. An entire row of trees went down like a band across the forest.

For the split second between the sight and the sound reaching him, Roman thought of loggers clear cutting, but that wasn't right. The new clear space was also clear of people and machines. The drop had been instant like a great, invisible weight had fallen onto the forest all at once.

In the midst of the larger, felled timber, Roman saw smaller pines bent down along their flexible trunks. He thought they might be pinned under the larger trees, but some were standing alone near clearings. It was as if the smaller trees were bowing in respect to some unseen force.

Roman cursed in Russian and said, "I should have listened to your crazed rantings about spirits more closely, Mother."

More individual trees crumbled around the edges of the band of destruction. Roman looked for a fissure or sink hole where the forest floor might be breaking over a magma pocket of some ancient, forgotten volcano, but there was nothing. The ground was whole.

Motion to the south drew his attention and he panned the binoculars. Another band of trees collapsed in the wake of the phenomenon. It was further from him and Roman could not see the exposed floor from his vantage this time. He could see the band was thinner this time, but miles longer.

He watched with his jaw open as thinner trees bowed slowly down from their tops.

"Show due respect to our invisible tiger master."

Roman heard a screaming roar build around him. He looked around for the source and then lowered the glasses.

The fighter raced over the top of the tower close enough to shake the entire structure. Roman thought he was going to be flung right out the opening. A mist of gooey film lighted on his skin and smelled like spilled kerosene. As he watched the fighter drift down toward the forest, Roman touched the sticky paste over his arms. "Jet fuel?"

The fighter hit the trees and clipped through the ones that were still standing before gliding into the space of the open band like it were a prepared landing strip. "Was this a military operation?"

He brought the lenses back up which were partially obscured by the film of spilt fuel from the air. Roman cursed in English. "That's not a Russian craft."

As he watched the plane hit the ground in a tumble over the fallen timber, Roman saw the smaller trees rise from their bow like they were raising their heads to watch the crashing enemy plane.

More crackles and falling trees traveled up the hill below him. Roman took his view off the plane and followed the path of falling trees approaching him. "Is that you, Tiger?"

Roman felt his legs grow heavy and he felt dizzy. The binoculars increased in weight until he finally let go of them and they pulled on the strap along the back of his neck.

The hatch slammed closed behind him and then ripped loose tumbling down the ladder. He heard the scream of metal on metal and Roman dropped to his knees. "What is happening?"

The tower collapsed around him and Roman was plunged into painful darkness.

Sean Grayson – West Memphis, Arkansas

Sean ran through the open door of the apartment, but then the ceiling came down. Sean barreled forward to keep from getting buried. He turned and saw beams down and burning over the doorway. An engulfed sofa from the apartment above sat on its side in flames.

Baker's voice hit the radio. "We have a man trapped inside."

The milk was spilled across the table. The cup rolled off, but seemed to fall it slow motion. It bounced on the kitchen tile with a click and then floated slowly back up cutting a trail through the smoke. This had to be one of those moments where time seemed to slow down.

"Up, up, and away," Sean said.

He ran down the hall, but then another collapse brought the ceiling down around him. The drywall warped into waves on both sides and exploded into powder and splinters. Sean dove forward toward the bathroom instead of back out of the collapse.

He shoved the chunks of wall off of him as he looked back at the burning debris which now filled the apartment. The chunks of wall lifted off of him and twirled in the air without landing again.

Sean could see through the missing section of wall into the kitchen. The balloon cup was still spinning in the air from its bounce creating a cyclone effect in the smoke. Now the plates, forks, and bits of food were dancing through the smoky air in the kitchen too.

Sean blinked and looked through the open face of the bathroom. The toothbrush floated by. As he watched, the shower curtain parted itself and lifted up in the air like it was being blown by a wind. A beam lay across the tub and he saw a small hand wave.

The boy's voice echoed in the tub. "It's on my leg. I can't move."

The tub had saved him from getting crushed, but Sean needed to get him out before they both burned. He stood and ran toward the bathroom.

He had that empty floating feeling again that signaled his life coming apart in a familiar way. This time though, Sean pushed off and his feet left the ground. His legs kicked up over his head and he spun once in the air before floating above the floor between the hallway and the bathroom.

He stared down at the boy in the tub. The kid stared back with eyes wide and his hands up at Sean. Sean wondered, *Am I already dead? Am I losing my mind?*

He had taken Oxy enough to hallucinate before. In rehab, the hallucinations had gotten really bad enough during withdrawals that they almost sent him to the hospital. Sean had pretended everything was fine, so that he wouldn't be found out as an addict outside the facility.

The kitchen table and burning sofa were doing tricks in the apartment too. The yellow tablecloth spread out along the top of the floating table like wings ready to fly away.

Sean swallowed and muttered. "Foster isn't the only one hitting the ceiling today."

He shook his head inside his helmet and mask. He reached out and grabbed a piece of wood sticking up from where the wall had broken. The board snapped in his hand and the piece floated away. He clawed at the air more until he caught a section of drywall. It crumbled into dozens of tiny asteroids that cut through the smoke in trails, but finally he got enough of a grip to pull himself forward.

Sean soared forward and down to the tub. He grabbed the beam and yanked with his feet up in the air behind him. It didn't budge. The boy was unconscious now.

Sean braced his feet against the tub and pulled with little hope that he could move the beam. It popped loose from where it was wedged in the tub and floated up like the kitchen table.

The boy floated up with his arms and legs out and Sean caught him. The ceiling came loose above them from the shifted beam. Sean watched the debris come down, but then pause and spread out in the air above them.

Sean kicked off the tub and floated through the air with the boy in his arms. He kicked off another section of wall in the hall. His boot went through, but he changed his direction and floated out through the wall of burning objects across the room. Sean swept them out of his path to avoid burning the boy.

He saw the cup still spinning and Sean whispered. "What now?"

It suddenly fell to the floor at full speed. The rest of the debris crashed down as well washing flame out across the carpet with the impact. Sean felt his own weight return and he shifted the boy's body to keep from landing on him. He slammed to his knees.

The entire building rumbled around him in its violent return to reality. Sean charged into one of the bedrooms as the apartment above came crashing completely in.

As the entire building shook, Sean kicked out the glass from the window. He clicked his radio and said, "This is Grayson. I'm at the window. Second floor. East side. I need an exit."

"We see you," Carter said over the radio. "I'm putting a portable ladder up now."

The top rung hit the window frame and Sean looked out to see Carter climbing. He took the boy from Sean and Sean climbed out too.

As they passed the boy off to paramedics, the ground rumbled again and Sean grabbed a lamppost to keep from floating away. The interior floors collapsed inside the brick shell with flame torching up through the windows. The companies blasted water into the ruined building to try to finish it off.

Sean turned and saw Carter staring at him. Sean realized he was still clutching the lamppost.

Carter tilted his head. "You okay, man?"

Sean let go of the post and pulled off his mask. "Yeah, I'm fine."

There was no chance that Sean was going to confess to hallucinating that he was flying.

They loaded up after the fire was doused and returned to the house. Back when Sean was married, he never talked to Tabby about the tough days. Now that he was dating Jenny, he tried not be closed off. She encouraged him to share and even vent when he needed. He wasn't sure he was ready to share this experience – whatever it was. He sensed beginning to lie now was a mistake, but he felt pulled by his fear.

Sean glanced at Carter who nodded at him and Sean looked away again.

As they entered the firehouse and unloaded, someone shouted. "What happened here?"

The other guys walked up and stared. Their trunks were overturned and busted open. Two bunks were tilted against the walls. Cabinets were open and the plates spilled on the floor. The skillet was across the room and the cold noodles ran down the wall in a greasy mess.

Lt. Foster came up last and said, "It wasn't like this when we left, right?"

"No, sir," Carter said. "Looks like that quake we felt wasn't from the building collapsing."

Foster said, "I told you Stroganoff for breakfast was a mistake, Grayson."

Sean swallowed and thought about the experience of flying through the fire. "Yes, sir."

The alarm sounded again and all the men groaned.

Foster shouted. "Replace oxygen tanks in a hurry and suit up. If you aren't broken, get ready to go."

5

Dr. Paulo Restrepo – Marlo-Pitts Observatory, Colombia

Dr. Paulo Restrepo leaned closer to the computer screen and scrolled between the images from the Australian observatory. He shook his head. He identified five in the middle of the sequence that were not even from the right year much less the correct time of year. Paulo wondered if they were testing him or were actively trying to sabotage his research. If it was a mistake, it was a spectacular one and he did not want to believe he was coordinating with people that were that incompetent.

He sent the message pointing out the slides that were mistakenly included and asked to be given the correct images for those time stamps.

Paulo was stopped in his tracks until he had the complete data. He leaned back in his chair and scratched at the gray in his beard. He stood and walked to the office window. The array for the telescope spread in a massive, reflective valley at the hollowed out top of the mountain several meters above him. Below he could see the outskirts of the village.

The university and larger sections of the city were around the highway on the far side of the mountain. *Too much light over there*, Paulo thought. On this side, the village was on a strict blackout order from the government at night. Just the other night, a floodlight had been installed by one of the villagers. An entire night of data was lost from a team of visiting German scientists. The month's schedule was completely off. One more delay and Dr. Restrepo's session would be cut short next. His grant would be at risk.

Paulo knew the spot where the light had been erected. He could see the tin roof and the bare pole where troops had cut down the light and detained the man. The Marlo-Pitts Observatory Array was big funding for the university and the Colombian government. They all took their funding seriously.

Likewise, they took success and failure seriously and Paulo needed his data.

He turned away from the window and scanned through public journal databases. He skipped past the abstract and even the data references to the raw data files. Most of it would be uncompiled and unusable for his purposes, but he was desperate. If he could imply some level of potential embarrassment for the Australians by simply appearing to be cross-referencing their findings, then maybe he could speed their reply with the information he really needed.

He leaned on his hand and his eyes drooped as he scanned through mountains of information that was largely unpublishable.

Paulo spotted some key image files from the reference points he needed uploaded from an observatory in Hawaii. He did a quick render to simply mark the points he needed in order to highlight the Australian mistake on the five frames of misplaced data.

The images came up rough and he narrowed his eyes. Paula actually put his fingers on the screen to trace out the points. He chewed at the inside of his mouth as he rough rendered them again. The rendering came up a second time identical to before. The data was being read correctly; it was just that the data couldn't be right.

Paulo initiated a more detailed imaging of the data. This couldn't be right. If anything, the Hawaiian numbers were further off than Australia. It was as if he was looking at an image of the sky from weeks, months, or years earlier. It wasn't the whole sky though.

Dr. Restrepo leaned in closer. He put his finger on the screen again. He zoomed in twice. There were afterimages. Along a certain line he was seeing two images of the same stars in two different positions. He would attribute it to a fault in their lens, but he had already found the anomaly from two different observatories without even truly looking for it.

Paulo stopped the data download and widened the data pull to include the sections of space outside the visual range of the distortion.

He searched through the databases and pulled every image from the time references from the key sectors of the sky that were available. It was not a lot of data, but it was a lot to fully image. He would need to contact the observatories to request all the data.

Paulo needed more hard drive space.

He dialed the director and waited. "Yes, sir, sorry to bother you. I need longer for my session this week. I desperately need that data … Yes, sir, I understand, but I wouldn't ask, if it wasn't vital. I do a lot for this observatory and I feel I've earned a little leeway … Yes, sir … Can I at least be granted more drive space between now and my session, so I can make the most of that time? … Yes, sir, right away, please … Thank you."

Dr. Paulo Restrepo smiled as he hung up. It was a dirty trick to play on the director under his current level of stress, but it got him what he needed. He would also now be less likely to bump Paulo's time.

Paulo opened up a wider allotment for his downloads and imaging and the process started moving faster. He licked his lips and realized if he found the distortions in the images from more sources, he was going to need to redirect his session toward a different section of sky.

He decided that he couldn't possibly have been the only one that identified a distortion in space that changed the visual references of the stars to their relative positions at a different point in time. He didn't even know of an anomaly that could do that.

Paulo opened his browser to search for news that would give him clues or show a pattern in occurrences. A particular one got his attention.

"New pill is created in Switzerland. European webnews article extract."

After retiring from a Chemical Engineering position in a company in Switzerland, Julien thought he should try to come up with one or two inventions that would help humankind. He also wanted to be remembered for his good deed after he was gone.

Julien and his three other retired and happy friends liked to meet once a month and talk about the old days and sports, followed by lots of laughing and lots of beer. They met in a small, charming restaurant on 8th Avenue in Geneva. The restaurant offered a delicious aged cheese as dessert and no one could say no to it. The only adverse effect was the flatulence it caused on the hosts.

Julien and his friends had so much flatulence at the end of the meal, it always ended up irritating guests on the tables nearby and the restaurant smelled noxious for some time.

So Julien had this novel idea - why not invent a pill that makes flatulence smells like chocolate?

Julien went back to his lab at home and worked hard on his new invention. The pill was ready after one week. He tried a couple of times and it worked perfectly on him. Now it was time to try it with his friends.

Julien arrived at the restaurant with a little box containing the pills. He explained to his friends how wonderful the pills were and each friend swallowed one.

After eating the cheese they waited. But little did they know the cheese chemistry combined with the pill started making them have uncontrollable, strong short bouts of flatulence.

To everyone's surprise, the gravity started to wane and the restaurant guests began to float gently, except for Julien and his friends, which were being propelled uncontrollably across the room at every burst from their bottoms, leaving in the air a fragrance of the finest chocolate."

Paulo chuckled.

As he searched online, most of the news was about earthquakes at various points on the Earth. A story about one in Arkansas and Tennessee in the United States caught his attention.

He gave up his search immediately and pulled out his cell phone. He got a "cell towers are busy" message. Paulo dialed a local number and let it ring once before he hung up.

He pulled up his e-mail and typed out a quick message to his daughter to see if she was alright.

6

Sean Grayson and Jenny Restrepo – West Memphis, Arkansas

Jenny Restrepo took out her phone and scrolled through her e-mail in the passenger's seat. Sean glanced over at her for a moment and turned his attention back on the road. Traffic inched forward. A spray of water blasted into the air from a busted water main. Sean could see the lights from the truck, but couldn't tell which company was handling the break while the city workers tried to repair it. They were outside his firehouse's territory, but with the quakes, they had been pulled all over the city.

Water rained down onto his windshield in a heavy wash as traffic pulled him forward and stopped him under the water. Sean turned his wipers on high and flipped on his headlights. He took off his sunglasses and stuck them in the center console as he squinted to see the taillights of the car in front of him.

"I'm going to get called back in on short rest," Sean said. "The city is a mess."

"They told you that already?" Jenny bent over her phone and thumbed in a message with expert speed.

"No, but I'm sure of it. They have every company out dealing with accidents and breaks all over. They are going to burn through every shift before my off time is up."

"That's too bad. Do you still want to plan on getting away?"

"I don't know," Sean said. He inched forward again and water thundered on the roof. "I might ought to hang close."

"Whatever you want, baby. We can go another time. I'll take off during the week in your next break, if I have to. We'll find something fun to do close by when we pick up your boys."

Sean smiled and put his hand on her knee just below the end of her shorts. Her skin was warm and smooth. He glanced at her and forward again. "Who are you texting?"

"E-mailing," She said. She shook her head still looking down at her phone. Her dark ponytail whipped back and forth over her neck and Sean swallowed. She was almost too beautiful to look at for too long. Sean thought, *she could do better; I couldn't, but she could.* She said, "My dad read about the earthquake on the Internet and is freaking out.

The cell towers are out in Colombia or something, so he had to e-mail instead of call."

"Did they have any trouble down there?" Sean asked.

Jenny squinted at him and laughed. "Why would they have trouble all the way down there from a little quake in Arkansas?"

Sean shrugged. He rolled forward out of the spray far enough to see the flares in his lane ahead. He turned the wheel to follow traffic toward the far shoulder. "I don't know. You said the cell towers were out."

"Oh, right." She shrugged and stuffed her phone back into the pocket of her shorts. He moved his hand off her knee as she rose up in the seat to get to her pocket. He watched how her body moved before looking back at the cars ahead. She said, "I don't know. He's up on that mountain out in the jungle, so that they are away from the lights. There is no telling what reception problems he's having. I told him I was just fine with a big, strong, redneck firefighter to protect me."

"Stop." He laughed. "I told you that is not a compliment and that word doesn't mean just anyone from the South."

She winked at him and blew a kiss. When she smiled, he shivered and looked back at the road. They edged past the firetruck on the shoulder, but Sean didn't bother to look to see which company it was.

Jenny said, "I went to school here for business admin. I know what a redneck is."

"A lot of rednecks in business administration?"

"A lot of them own the businesses."

Sean nodded. "You should have just told your dad that everything was fine or it wasn't as bad as the news made it look. That would comfort him more than telling him your boyfriend was protecting you from earthquakes."

Jenny laughed. "Maybe so, but it was kind of bad, wasn't it? I don't want to lie to him. That fire in the apartment sounded awful. I saw the pictures. I'm terrified thinking you were in there before it fell down."

Sean sighed. "Yeah, it got hairy. I had to get a little boy out that tried to hide in a tub. We almost missed him and then I had to get a beam off of him once we found him."

"How many did it take to lift it off?"

Sean cleared his throat. "Just me, I guess."

"Oh?" She made a show of fanning herself with her hand. "My big, strong, superhero redneck boyfriend. He is so powerful."

Sean poked her in the ribs with one of his fingers. She squirmed and giggled. Sean watched her for a moment and looked back forward blinking.

After a few seconds of creeping forward past the water main repair, she said, "It sounds like it was very scary. Are you okay?"

He nodded and swallowed without looking away from the road. "Yeah. It was burning before the quake. Then, the tremor must have brought the whole thing down. Me and the boy were the last ones out. They still don't know how many were still inside."

"That's terrible." Jenny covered her mouth. "Did you feel it when it started? What was it like being in there during an earthquake?"

Sean thought about the objects floating, him lifting the beam like it had no weight, and kicking down the hallway in the air through floating fire like he was moving through space. He opened his mouth to tell her, but then closed it again. He wanted to, but he did not trust himself. He did not want her to see him as in trouble or in need of saving. He swallowed and took a deep breath. Even as he felt that it was a mistake to do so, he pushed the truth back down away from his mouth and left it unsaid.

Sean said, "You know me. I'm a brave, redneck firefighter. Nothing scares me."

She swatted his shoulder and stuck out her tongue. "It is okay to be scared. It keeps you alive sometimes."

"Sometimes," Sean said.

The traffic broke up and he drove forward again. Sean turned off on a side road and continued on.

"Where are we going?" she asked.

"I need gas."

He pulled into the station and edged up to the pump. Sean stepped out and fished through his wallet for a credit card with room on it to cover the fill-up. An advertisement sign at the pump read "Pre-order your android companion now!"

"We have to use cash." Jenny leaned out her window.

Sean looked down at his wallet and back at her. Maybe she knew more about him than he realized. "Why?"

She pointed up to the pump. "The sign."

A piece of copy paper was taped over the credit card reader with what must have been half a roll of scotch tape. It read simply: DOWN. Pay $cash$ inside.

Sean nodded and closed his wallet. "Well, there you go."

"Hold on," Jenny said. "I want a snack. I'll go in with you."

He leaned on the pump as he waited on her to get out. "I thought you were into eating healthy and natural."

"I didn't say what kind of snack."

"It's a gas station. They only have so much."

She closed her door and looked back at the open window. "Did you want to roll up and lock it?"

Sean snorted and turned away. "Nobody wants what I've got. Come on."

She fell in beside him and hooked her arm through his. Jenny leaned up and kissed him on the cheek before she whispered. "I want what you've got."

He felt gooseflesh travel over his body. He almost told her that she could do better. He stopped himself because she did not like that joke. She didn't like anything that he said that put himself down. That eliminated a lot of his usual humor. Maybe she was perfect for him after all.

They entered the convenience store section of the station and stopped short. Sean and Jenny looked at each other and back at the shelves. One man stood behind the counter. He was older with a thick mustache and he scribbled out in long hand down the page of a spiral notebook. He huffed and turned the page with angry resolve. Another clerk, a younger man with a ponytail, swept busted packages up in the aisle and used what looked like a snow shovel to dump them into a trashcan sitting in the middle of the floor. Many packages were head lice medications.

"What happened here?" Jenny called out.

The younger clerk shook his head and kept shoveling. The older man glared at them and then back down at his notebook. "Quake turned the store upside down. Cash only for gas."

Sean approached the counter and took out two fives and a ten. "Twenty on pump three."

"What kind?"

"Regular, please."

"Thank you for your business." The man went back to scribbling. Sean saw he was listing inventory and numbers. He assumed it was for a damage report.

"The quake knocked out your credit card reader."

"No, satellite."

Sean tilted his head. "The quake knocked out the satellite? The dish you mean?"

The man raised his eyes from the notebook and glared at Sean. Sean expected him to yell, but the clerk's voice went softer. "No, satellites are in space. Couple satellites in space were knocked out of orbit. Now credit cards won't read until other satellites take over. Cash only for now. Okay."

"Yeah, no problem. Sorry."

The man waved his pencil hand and went back to writing.

Sean turned to Jenny. "You getting something? I'm about to go pump."

She looked around the floor and shook her head. "Think I'll wait until we get home."

Sean nodded. He looked up at the banks of hanging florescent lights and thought the station was lucky none of those came down. It seemed odd to Sean that none of them would have shook loose in an earthquake.

As he approached the door with Jenny, he saw more packages of pink donuts and bags on chips sitting balanced on top of the lights. He paused at the door. *What kind of quake could shake hard enough to toss items off the shelf high enough to land on the lights?*

Sean whispered. "Turned the store upside down." *Like they floated up there*, he thought. The gooseflesh was back, but not in the good way when Jenny whispered to him.

"Sean? What's wrong?"

He startled and turned away from the lights. "Nothing. Just trying to figure out what's going on with the world. Nothing I can explain yet."

She rubbed her hand across his back. Her fingernails through his shirt made him shiver. "As long as you remember that you don't have to figure it all out by yourself."

7

Captain Michael Strove and Roman Nikitin – Russia

Michael climbed back up the angle of the wing to the cockpit of the fighter. His knee slipped and he fell flat on his belly against the damaged skin of the craft. He felt every ache, bruise, and wretched joint from the crash that should have killed him.

If he didn't hurry, the charges he laid around the stress points and ports of the downed plane would take him up with it and he would fail to eliminate the proprietary tech in the cockpit itself.

He growled at his own pain and forced himself back up. Michael crawled up and forward. He broke the ends of the burners and saw the phosphorus flares blast out of the tubes. He dropped them inside before they could burn his fingers off and slid back down the wing to the churned soil, barely avoiding the sharp edges of bent metal in his path.

His knees threatened to give out, but he hobbled into a run dodging around the excavated root systems of massive trees which seemed too far from the path of his crash to be his fault. Michael hurt too badly to climb over the timber so he worked his way around as much of it as he could to put barriers between him and the coming firestorm.

The light burst up from the plane white hot. Michael leaned against the trunk of a tree that was still standing and turned to look even though he knew that he shouldn't and knew that he was probably still too close. He was on foreign ground without permission with tense relations at the worst time in a plane that could not be allowed to be found. He was a pilot burning up his own craft and taking to foot with nowhere to go and no way to get there.

For now, he was watching it all burn. It wasn't until he stopped that he considered the possibility that the intense heat might set the entire forest ablaze. *Add environmental tragedy to the news story of an American pilot invading Russia*, Michael thought.

The phosphorous blaze channeled up out of the broken cockpit like a geyser of flame as it incinerated the controls within. Data, computers, and polymer components melted into their base compounds to hide the secrets that they held. The data burn proceeded perfectly, but Michael also knew he was announcing his position in the brightest way possible.

31

They could spot him for miles, if they didn't already have him pinpointed and weren't already on their way. He had drifted across miles of Russian territory unconscious for much of it. He imagined he had been as large as a saucer on their radar the whole way in. As he considered it, he was surprised that they hadn't shot him down themselves. Michael remembered the wild distortions in the northern lights and the malfunctions in his plane that seemed to strike his Russian shadows at the same moment. He wondered if the effect had scrambled Russian radar and launchers in some manner too.

The charges around the seams of the plane lit up and Michael ducked down. The explosions blasted downward driving the force into the craft itself. Michael felt the vibration like a quake through the ground. It shook him hard enough that he suspected it might show up on a seismograph, if a station were close enough. It had been a mysterious weight that had pulled him down and the weight of directed charges that finished the job.

Michael stood and saw the melting remains of his cockpit with the plane blasted away around it. Several pieces were driven down into the soil that was blackened and smoldering. Most of the pieces were not big enough to hold in two hands. The Russians might be able to get hold of something that let them know what kind of plane they were dealing with even if they wouldn't be able to reconstruct it themselves. It would have to be good enough now.

He limped away and used the sun to guide himself roughly east. He had no way of knowing how far, but there was water somewhere in this direction. The U.S. hadn't had time to plan an extraction even if they intended to do one, but Michael had little other option, so the poor option would have to do.

He took to a rise and limped up between rocky outcroppings. He considered going around as the slope became steeper, but he figured the vantage point might be useful once he reached the top, even if it only showed him how screwed he really was.

As he emerged on the first tilt of flat ground, he spotted the remains of a tower. A couple of the metal legs stabbed up at the sky as the rest of the structure settled in a pile of debris in front of him. The remains of the metal ladder twisted around the outside of the whole thing like an angry snake. He couldn't tell how long ago it had collapsed, but the rust spots and stress points on the metal led him to believe the tower had been abandoned and forgotten long ago.

He turned and looked out over the land. He saw a river to the north and a spark of light beyond it that gave a hint that something might lie beyond. Michael might not have any choice in the end, but for now he would avoid people, so north and its hint were out.

The rest of the land spread empty as far as he could see in every other direction. He felt alone, isolated, and vulnerable. Large swatches of fallen trees scarred the land in broad stripes, but only served to mark the vast distances for him. The piles of lumber with the tops still on and green made him think this was not result of purposeful cutting.

The smell of fresh, split pine drifted thick on the wind to his nostrils and unnerved him a little. He thought of live trees at Christmas time back home with his brother and his parents back when they were strong, alive, and whole in mind. Here with the smell this strong and fresh, he didn't know what it meant and he didn't much like not knowing.

He heard a voice behind him and Michael spun around. His hand went to his side and he realized he had not retrieved a sidearm before bailing from the craft and destroying it. It hadn't been anywhere near him at the time.

The voice moaned and babbled in Russian again and Michael honed in on it echoing out from the debris of the tower. "Not so abandoned after all."

"Hello? Is someone there? I'm trapped and hurt."

Michael swallowed. He needed to go. He did not have the tools or strength for a rescue. And he certainly did not have the authority to take one on in the midst of the Russian wilderness after scuttling his top secret aircraft. The right move was to leave and keep going. Yet, he was still standing and facing the voice trapped under the broken metal. It was another man down even if it wasn't his man.

"Do you understand me?" Michael said. He heard his voice shake. Even his words were unsure of this decision.

"Yes, please, help me. I can't move, but I can see light. I just need my legs freed."

Michael took a step forward, but stopped short of the angry snake ladder. "Are you bleeding? Is the metal cutting into your legs at all? I don't want to pull it off and have you bleed to death."

"I don't understand what you ... no, I'm not bleeding. Just trapped. I can move my toes. No breaks. Just trapped. Help me, please."

Michael ducked under the bent ladder and walked up the slope of the sheet metal. "Keep talking. I don't want to step on you and make it worse."

It's a little late to not make it worse, Michael thought.

"I just saw your shadow pass, man. I can't reach the opening with my hand, but it is right there now."

Michael knelt down and grabbed the edge of the sheet metal. "Hold on."

"There. I see your hands."

Michael lifted the first piece and rolled it off the pile with ease. He saw the Russian's hands and his face. His nose and cheek were bloodied. Michael didn't know how hurt the man was. He was wearing a greenish uniform that could have been army. "Are you Russian army?"

"No, I'm a ... tree ... I watch ... A ranger ... forest ranger? I watch the trees and they forget I exist."

Michael nodded. He pulled up on the metal folded over the top of the man. It groaned and gave a little, but would not lift. "Am I hurting you?"

"No, it is lifting off, but not enough. I can pull myself out, but I need more lift, man."

"Hold on." Michael climbed off the side and walked around the pile.

"Don't leave me here, man, please."

"I'm not. Trust me."

The Russian sighed and nodded. "Not much choice, but you had a choice. Thank you, man."

"You can thank me by not shooting me when I get you loose."

He said, "No, no shoot. No gun. I only use it for hunting and it is back at the ... house."

Michael picked up a pipe, but it wasn't long enough. He tossed it and kept searching. "A forest ranger that shoots the animals. That's new."

"I'm in this job ... ugh, exiled. They leave me out here because of my family. It is a punishment job. You understand?"

Michael picked up a longer pipe and climbed up under the ladder again. "So you are here alone?"

He looked from the pipe to Michael. "Don't kill me. You don't have to."

Michael looked down at the pipe. "No. I'm not."

He wedged it under the metal sheet and levered it up. "Not enough. More."

"I'm trying."

"What's your name?"

Michael paused, but then kept levering. "Captain Michael Strove, United States Airforce."

"You are far from home, man."

"I know. I crashed. I'm in trouble."

"I'm Roman Nikitin. I spend my whole life in trouble. No problem. Captain Michael."

Michael levered up and braced his shoulder under the pipe. "Crawl out, if you can. I can't hold it forever."

Roman shuffled out from under the metal and pulled his knees up to his chest as he rubbed his legs. "Oh, that hurts."

"Are you legs broken?"

"I don't think so. Where are you going?"

Michael stood and took a step back.

Roman rolled up to sitting. "I won't report you. I'll help you. I owe you. You could have left me."

Michael looked east. "I was over the Bering Strait. I need to get back to the coast, if I can."

Roman shook his head. "You mean the Sea of Okhotsk?"

"Okhotsk?" Michael shook his head. "No, I was in international water before ... I had a malfunction. I was pushed over land and crashed here. How far to the coast?"

Roman blinked and shook his head. "You are hundreds of kilometers from the coast of Okhotsk. The Bering Strait is over more land hundreds of kilometers past that. Unless you got another plane, you aren't getting there."

"I'm not on the peninsula?" Michael rubbed at his forehead.

Roman thought and shook his head. "No. Mainland. Deep, far mainland. Taiga forest, Captain Michael."

Michael backed away from the debris. "Maybe you can show me to the closest prison and save me some time."

"My house … cabin was an old listening station. Maybe you can connect the radio and get a signal out from there that your people could pick up. Maybe."

Michael stared at Roman. "Why would you help me do that?"

"I know what it is like to be in trouble and have someone help you."

Michael nodded.

The sounds of helicopter blades filled the air. They turned and saw three black helicopters crossing the river and flying low toward them. They veered west toward Michael's crash.

"I need to go," Michael said.

"That's not good for either of us," Roman said. "Help me up. I help you hide. We need to go … east."

Michael helped Roman down the slope of the debris. He staggered and Michael braced him under his shoulder. They limped a couple steps, but then the tones of the choppers changed and they turned to look out over the hill.

One of the three spun in a circle before dropping quickly. The others wavered, but then veered toward the ground.

Michael whispered. "What's happening?"

A wave of falling trees crackled across the land and traveled toward the rise as the trees marked the motion by breaking and falling in time.

Roman said, "Lay down?"

"What?"

"On the ground, Captain Michael. Hurry, man."

Michael got to his knees and lowered Roman off his shoulder to the patch of grass under them. Leaves rained down around them. The trees groaned as they strained under their own weight.

Michael tried to look up, but his neck hurt. He felt something push on his shoulders and he actually turned to see what it was. He slammed to the ground on his side facing Roman. The grass folded flat to the Earth so that Michael was looking Roman in the eyes. Michael tried to push himself up, but couldn't.

"What's happening?" Michael grunted.

Roman's voice answered strained and breathless. "Invisible tigers, I think."

8

Holden Grayson – Alberton Elementary School, West Memphis, Arkansas

Holden Grayson stared at the grass on the hill above the playground. He was next to the monkey bars as kids swung across hand over hand behind him. He held onto the post and stared at the hill.

The wind was blowing from the front of the school toward the teacher's parking lot. The grass seemed to disobey the wind. It folded back and pointed defiantly at the sky. A few blades broke free of the Earth and even with the wind pushing at their sides they twisted and launched themselves upward into the sky. Holden watched until the sun dazzled his eyes and he lost the rebellious sky grass.

Holden Grayson tried his best to obey as often as he could. It was harder since his mother and father split. Parents were supposed to stay together swaying with the wind like the grass on the hillside in a pattern that made sense. But sometimes they pulled loose and flew apart in ways that made no sense at all. Holden understood how wind worked, but he did not understand how his parents worked now. Sometimes their rules for him were different from each other and they were hard to follow. One was pushing while the other was pulling. And sometimes they switched.

Holden was eight and that was old enough to notice when things weren't right. His brother Grant was four and didn't really remember the world before their parents split. He also did not remember dad's trouble with anger and taking the pills that made him sick. They thought Holden did not know, but he remembered and the sadness from remembering pushed at his insides and pulled at his heart.

One of the kids on the diamond at the far end of the playground gave the red kickball a ringing boot high over the heads of the kids scattered through the infield. Something about that rubbery ping sound reminded Holden of the playground. All play was contained in that sound of a sneaker kicking a ball. Holden turned to watch it float and hang in the air. It was one heck of a kick, but the ball was getting tricky and floating instead of falling. Holden watched it spin on its own invisible axis in the air like some angry, red planet. The other kids ran under it waiting for it to fall. From their perspective, it was a high hanging kick. They were not seeing the dark magic Holden saw in its refusal to fall. The kicker was almost home with his fists raised in double pumping victory. The ball drifted down slowly and stubbornly to the hands of the defensive players.

Holden looked back at the kids navigating the monkey bars. Their feet swung up and the kids hung by their hands almost horizontal with their legs defying weight and gravity.

A kid on the sidewalk beside the wall of the school flicked a marble. It bounced off a cat's eye and hopped up off the concrete. The green glass orb hovered in the air with the kid staring, his jaw unhinged. At least someone else was seeing it too. That was something.

Something was strange on the playground today. It was the sort of thing that adults either praised kids from their imagination for telling or scolded them for making up fibs.

"Push and pull." Holden whispered.

He felt light and barely connected to the ground himself. Holden gripped the support of the monkey bars tighter trying to keep himself earthbound. He might run along hopping like he was on the Moon and then one, great leap could send him flying over the Moon like the cow in the nursery rhyme.

Holden looked for more evidence of the disobedient world and spotted his mother leaning on the fence next to the front parking lot. Uncle Carter's car was behind her. Carter was probably inside. They might have already picked up Grant from daycare. They were going camping as a family, Mom had said. She meant everyone except Dad. Uncle Carter was Dad's friend and worked with him at the firehouse saving people from burning. Now Carter was acting more like mom's friend and less like Dad's friend.

"Pushing Dad and pulling Mom."

His mom waved and Holden waved back. His hand still felt too light in the strange air of the playground. Holden kept his grip on the monkey bar pole.

He saw his father at the other end of the front fence of the playground. His dad was waving thinking Holden had been waving at him. This was normally Dad's weekend, but they had switched for the camping trip, Mom had said. She might not have told Dad since they almost never talked.

They had not seen each other yet, so they were both smiling. They didn't know yet that there needed to be a push/pull like they usually did with each other. It was weird seeing them both smiling together at the same time. It felt fragile like the moment could float away at any time.

Holden let go of the playground equipment and hoped for the best. "Pulling me. Pushing each other."

Holden ran toward the fence. He did not fly away from the Earth like he feared, but he felt lighter and faster than normal. Maybe the magic on the playground wasn't all bad.

Mom and Dad both moved toward the center not noticing each other. They were still smiling. It was like they were still together except that Dad wasn't sick anymore and mom wasn't angry at him. The playground was magic. Holden ran faster to try to outrun the pushing force that normally built between them.

They saw each other. The smiles faded. They were both talking at once. The lightness left as the strange magic faded around Holden. He felt his weight return and marbles, and children, and kick balls dropped with normal gravity again.

His feet and body felt heavy as he slammed into the chain link fence. It raddled with a harsh hiss. Mom and Dad came together on both sides of Holden on the opposite side of the fence, but he felt the strong push between them.

9

Sean Grayson and Tabitha Grayson – Alberton Elementary School, West Memphis, Arkansas

Tabitha said, "Holden, go wait in the car with your brother and Carter. I'll be there in a moment."

"I need my school bag," Holden said.

"We got it." Tabitha was staring at Sean as she spoke. "I already checked you out. Everything is in the car."

Sean felt heat in his cheeks. He glanced at Jenny in the passenger seat of his car. He looked over and saw Carter in the driver's seat of his own car. Carter looked away as soon as Sean spotted him. Grant waved from the backseat and Sean waved back. "This is my weekend, Tabby."

Tabitha sighed. "I sent you an e-mail. I left you three voice messages. We switch weekends all the time. I need you to respond to me though."

"I was working. So was Carter. If he knew about it, he could have said something."

Tabitha shook her head. "It's not Carter's job to pass messages between us."

"It's not his job to pretend to be raising my sons and taking them on trips on my weekend either."

Tabitha sucked in a deep breath and pointed at Sean's chest. She stopped and looked at Holden still staring over the fence at them. "Holden? Car."

Holden looked at his father. "Dad?"

Sean sighed and said, "Do what your mother says, son. We're talking. I'll see you when you get back from your trip."

"Are you sure, Dad?"

I'm anything but sure. I'm not sure about one thing in this world anymore including whether gravity holds us to the ground. How would you like to hear that from your crazy father, son? Sean saw Holden staring into his eyes and he felt broken inside. "I'm sure. Tell Carter I said, hello. Okay?"

Holden left them at the fence and walked toward the gate. "Okay, Dad. See you after the trip."

Holden had run to the fence, but he walked with his head down toward the gate. The difference was not lost on Sean.

"So, he asks your permission to do what I say?" Tabitha took hold of the fence and turned away.

In profile, Sean could see her jaw working and the muscles flexing as she chewed on nothing. Sean had seen that a lot in the years where he was hiding his addiction, the stretch when he was caught, but still pretending he was hiding it, and in the final days where he was justifying it and Tabitha was backed into a corner holding onto the kids with one hand and the house with the other as Sean destroyed himself and everything around him. He equated that flexing jaw with the terror of a woman feeling like everything would fly away at any moment. He was surprised she didn't leave sooner.

Sean looked toward the car and made eye contact with Jenny. She looked concerned. He turned his head away from her gaze the way Carter had done when he met Sean's gaze. Sean did not like looks of concern. They reminded him of secrets getting discovered. Looks of concern reminded him of lying and hiding. They brought up memories of being less of a man than he was supposed to be. The looks made him feel like he was inflated – only a man on the outside, but full of empty air inside.

Sean thought about floating through the halls during the fire and wondered if his mind was coming apart from the damage of past drug abuse and unresolved guilt. He had told no one about the moment in the fire yet. He was back to lies and secrets again. That was a tougher addiction to beat than the pills.

Tabitha stopped clenching her jaw and shook her head. "Classic."

"What do you mean by that?"

"He still worships you and puts the weight of everything that went wrong on my shoulders."

"Who? Holden? What are you talking about, Tabby?"

"Grant too now. You are the fun daddy and I am the every day rule keeper mommy. I guess nothing has really changed on that, so I should be used to it by now."

Sean shook his head. "What does this have to do with anything? Are you trying to punish me for everything in the past with a surprise canceling of my weekend? Is that it?"

"No, I tried to call."

"Then, why are you throwing this in my face because of your miscommunication? I couldn't check my phone while I had a burning building falling in around me as I ran out with a hurt kid in my arms. Things have been busy. You heard about the earthquake?"

"Yes, I heard. Of course I did. That's not what I'm saying."

"I almost died," Sean said. "Carter had to pull me out while everything was coming down."

"Not the first time for that either." Tabitha was back to clenching her jaw.

"You never get tired of throwing the past up in my face even when it is irrelevant to why we are standing here now."

"That's exactly why we are standing here passing the kids back and forth when we live a couple blocks from each other. And you are best friends with my boyfriend."

"That nonsense is far from my fault, Tabby. That's on you." Sean glanced at Carter's car again. Holden and Grant were pulling back and forth between some toy in the back seat. The blue sky obscured them to where they were just shapes – almost not there at all. They were fighting hard enough to shake the car from side to side, but Carter said nothing and just stared out the window away from Sean like the trees beyond the playground were the most interesting things in the world – like at any moment they might jump out of the dirt and start dancing for him, if he just kept watching. Sean said, "And it's on him."

"I'm sure your frat of friendly firemen are giving him hell for it."

Sean took a deep breath. "Yeah, the guys get a little put off when one of their own thinks its okay to take up with someone else's wife. There is kind of an unwritten code against that sort of thing, you can imagine."

"I'm not your wife, Sean. I don't belong to you."

"No. I don't think that you are or that you do, Tabby. I can only go with the plan we have, not the changed plan that never gets to me."

She blinked and tears leaked from her rapidly reddening eyes. She was a fast crier. It came on her suddenly. Even the few times it wasn't his fault, Sean felt tightness in his chest when her tears erupted. She would get the looks of concern from passing strangers and he would get the angry looks of a man that deserved to be accused. Often, he did deserve it and that made it worse.

For now, he did not want her returning to the car looking upset. He could care less what Carter thought of it, but he did not want the boys to see mommy upset because of Daddy again.

There was no fixing it though. If Sean knew the first thing about keeping her from being upset, they wouldn't be standing here now.

Sean said, "Holden isn't choosing me over you. He did what you said. He was just confused because of the miscommunication. That's all. They're good kids. They love you. They talk about you the whole time they are with me."

She cried harder. Sean nodded. *Yeah, I'm terrible at this*, he thought.

Tabitha wiped at her face with the back of her hand. "They do the same to me about you only I have to hear it longer."

"I can't help that."

"I'm just so mad at you."

"I can't help that either."

"No, I mean, I'm mad at you for getting better."

Sean huffed and shrugged. "Well, I suppose I could relapse or die. I came close this morning ... to dying, I mean."

She shook her head. "That's not what I'm saying. You pulled your life together and became a better person – started treating people better. Jenny gets the better you. I stuck by you and fought all those years until I was broken and slinked out a couple blocks away with the kids. She gets the version of you that I always hoped you would be, Sean, but I couldn't last any longer. She gets that and Carter gets me still broken and wrung out from it all. You are on the upswing and I'm still flattened by it. Carter gets the shell of a woman and Jenny gets Sean Grayson whole again. It makes me angry that you couldn't be that while we were still together and I was still whole."

Sean blinked on tears now and looked toward the ground. "I'm still a shell of a man, Tabby; I just look real from the outside."

Tabitha reached a hand out toward his chest. It shocked him and he stumbled back a step before she made contact. She dropped her hand back to her side. "I'm sorry for the mix-up. We'll work out the switch after we get back from camping at Black Fork. I'm sure the boys will forget the camping trip and talk about whatever adventure you take them on."

She was smiling, but it was tight and uncomfortable. Sean took another step back. "You're not supposed to camp up in Black Fork. It's only for hiking."

"Don't start, Sean." She turned away and walked toward Carter's car with her head down.

Sean whispered. "I'm not starting."

But she was too far away to hear. He turned his back and leaned both hands on the playground fence. He took several deep breaths feeling like he was the one wrung out now.

A car door opened behind him. "Sean?"

He turned his head and Jenny stood beside the open passenger door. The look of concern on her face made him feel heavy and tired. He held up one finger. "Everything is fine. Give me just a minute."

"What happened? Is this not your weekend?"

He shook his head. "I'll explain in a minute. Give me just a minute."

She nodded and sat back in the passenger's seat of Sean's car with her door still open. He stared for a moment longer. *No, this is certainly not my weekend. If you knew what ride you were signing up for, would you have still gotten in my car, Jenny?*

He turned away and looked out over the playground.

"Hey, Firefighter Sean." A kid Sean didn't recognize was waving and Sean waved back.

Sean and Carter had done fire safety programs at Holden's school for years – even back before Carter was with Tabitha.

One of the teachers waved and Sean waved back. He was thankful she didn't come over. She probably saw the exchange and wanted no part of it. West Memphis wasn't so big that people didn't know which conversations to avoid between exes. People knew which men were in the process of burning their lives down around them even if they didn't know every dirty detail yet.

He heard an engine rev and turned in time to watch Carter drive away with the family that Sean had pushed away.

Motion in the corner of his eye caught his attention and he looked back over the playground. Blades of grass twisted and danced in the air as they fell slowly back to the ground. It was only a couple at first, but then the falling grass rained down on the playground like confetti. The teachers and students stopped and looked up at the sky. Sean stared up

44

at the sun, but saw nothing in the empty sky that could explain the falling grass. He had not been watching and had missed how the dance of the grass had begun. Maybe Carter was wise to keep his eyes on the trees.

10

Michael Strove and Roman Nikitin – Russia

Micheal put his back to the truck of a tree. Roman pulled away from him and did the same at another trunk. Michael snuck a look around and saw light breaking the horizon. Morning was coming and he was exhausted from dodging the search parties all night. Darkness had covered them some, but he would be surprised if at least some of the Russian soldiers pursuing did not have night vision or heat sensors.

Michael and Roman had been running, hiding, and zigzagging all night.

His feet crunched under him like snow. He looked down in the growing light and saw he was standing on piles of shaved bark. He looked up. The trees were shaved clean nearly all the way up. Larger branches near the top had broken off as well. It looked like they had weathered a terrible storm, but one that pulled straight down instead of sideways.

"How close are we to your station?" Michael asked.

Roman slid down the trunk and sat. "Far. We are going the wrong way again, Captain Michael."

Michael bit his lip. "Do you not know where we are going, Roman?"

"I know. We have just had to keep circling away from them. We need to hook back … ugh, east."

Michael nodded. "Do you think they know where we are headed?"

"I don't see how. We keep going the wrong way. It is the perfect plan."

Michael sniffed and shook his head. "Do I need to let you go? If they catch you with me, you could be in big trouble."

Roman shook his head. "As long as we are not caught, I am safe. We need to keep going."

Michael looked east again. "It's daylight. We should probably find a place to hide and rest."

"Then, let's go, Captain Michael." Roman started to stand, but winced as he put weight on his ankle.

Michael crossed over and knelt in front of Roman. "Are you hurt?"

"Yes, I was in a tower crushed by an invisible tiger from space, man."

"Your ankle, I mean."

Roman dropped back to sitting. "It is getting all fat. It only hurts when it twists from side to side. It is weak."

"Swollen," Michael said. "Sprained. Stretch out your leg for me."

Roman extended his knee. Michael started gathering small sticks and pulled a section of cord from one of his pockets.

"Why did you help me?" Roman asked.

"What do you mean?" Michael took out a knife and cut off a section of cord before putting the knife away.

"You did not know I would be helping you. You needed to avoid discovery," Roman said, "Why risk it on me?"

"My brother Carter saves people." Michael braced the sticks around Roman's ankle and wrapped the cord around them.

"You trying to better up Brother Carter by saving a dirty Russian, Captain Michael."

Michael tied the cord off and tested the sticks. He continued wrapping the cord higher on the splints. "No, not trying to be better. Maybe just as good. He is a firefighter. He saves people every day. I thought maybe I should do it at least one day."

"I picked the right day to meet you then," Roman said.

"Why did you help me?" Michael asked.

"You saved a dirty Russian in a smooshed tower, man. I owe you."

"No, but you still didn't have to risk your freedom by running with me. Why are you sticking with me?"

Roman looked away. "My mother is Jewish."

Michael stared at Roman for a moment. He went back to tending the ankle. "Are you trying to be better than your mother?"

Roman laughed. "Not possible, man. Well, she was nice to our family. She could be mean to others. But still. We had trouble with people and she kept her secrets. She wanted democracy like in Israel or in America, but for Russia. She thought Russia was empty democracy. One thing on the outside, but nothing to it inside. She made my father lose his hair with all her talk. Our family got in trouble and I was sent out here. I was too unimportant to really punish, so I only got this half punishment."

"So, you helped me for democracy?" Michael asked.

"I learned English and Yiddish because my mother loved what those countries had – America and modern Israel," Roman said. "I learned English better. America is more flashy. I like the TV, man. When you helped me, it was like all the American hero men in the TV shows. Like all of the men your brother Carter is, right? It stopped being flashy for me and felt real – like something on the outside and the inside like my mother always wanted, but never got while she was alive. It is probably still a mistake to help you, Captain Michael, but that is why. This is all the fault of my Jewish mother and Brother Carter."

Michael laughed and tied off the end of the cord. "Okay, does that hurt?"

"No, it is side to side that hurts."

"Let's try to stand up," Michael said and pulled Roman to his feet.

He pressed down on his ankle. "Feels good. Brother Carter could have done no better if he were stranded in Russian wilderness."

Michael took Roman's arm over his shoulder. "No wilderness hopefully. Just the big city of West Memphis. Let's see if we can find a spot to hide."

"Oh, wow, Brother Carter lives in Elvis's town. He has it better than you right now, Captain Michael."

Michael nodded. "Elvis was the other side of the river, but close enough. Yeah, he does have it better right now probably."

11

Dr. Paulo Restrepo – Marlo-Pitts Observatory, Colombia

Data was pouring into Dr. Restrepo's e-mail and file server faster than he could organize it. It was as if he was the only one asking the questions and observers around the world were dying to tell someone. Paulo swallowed as he scanned through the images and partial reports. *Maybe I'm the only one who is listening,* he thought.

The director spoke behind Paulo and startled him as Dr. Restrepo had forgotten he was even there. It had been so long since he had spoken as he stared over Paulo's shoulder. "I'm suspending all other observations until further notice. You have all the hard drive space you need. Call me again when you know something."

Paulo answered. "I know we may be in serious trouble."

"I surmised that. I'm going to set up some calls. When you are ready to present to authorities, let me know."

Paulo did not look, but heard the director walking to the door. "Which authorities? Which governments?"

"All of them, Doctor." The director closed the door leaving Paulo alone with his thoughts and data.

He opened a separate Internet connection to search details on the earthquake near where his daughter lived. She had assured him more than once that everything was fine. Paulo knew that it certainly was not okay on a cosmic scale and probably she was withholding details from him on a local scale too.

As he scrolled through disconcerting pictures from Arkansas, he found details of other quake activity around the world that concerned him more. The patterns were more obvious when he had the data to tell him what to be looking for.

In China, Russia, the Middle East, and Eastern Europe, the reports were of crushing G forces that were bringing down buildings and trees. Planes had been pushed down from the sky in what Paulo now knew to be an unprecedented gravitational anomaly.

In Spain, West Africa, the United States, and Central America, reports of objects floating and weightlessness were filling the Internet.

He scrolled through more examples. An observation post in Antarctica reported rare tidal waves striking the ice shelf. The waves appeared to be an accumulation of three separate ocean quakes. The smaller, but still deadly individual waves were reported in Chile, South Africa, and India.

He turned back to his data. Paulo drummed his fingers. He started running his own calculation from the raw data of separate, global sources. A wave passing through the Earth's crust itself could create quakes.

"Pressing down as it pushing through China," he said aloud. "Pulling up as it came out through my daughter's living room?"

He shook his head. *The Earth rotates as it revolves. We would be in a different relative orientation and different sides would face the oncoming wave, if it has an extra-solar source which it must be.*

Paulo took a pencil and scribbled a separate calculation on a notebook as the computer ran more complex numbers for him. He figured how many relative kilometers the Earth would travel in orbit before the same side of the planet were facing the same relative point in space. He became more specific and drew stars outside his numbers as dots giving them initials for his rough star chart.

"Eastern hemisphere," he said. "Entry point … each time would be facing …" He slid the pencil point out to a dot marked AC.

Paulo squinted. He pulled up the distortion images and traced his finger over the band of incorrect space representing the incoming gravitational waves. "Double stars," he said as he looked along the edge of the distortion.

He flipped back and forth between five images in a cycle. "Double stars … and missing stars."

He returned to his scribbled calculations and drew curved lines out from the dot marked AC like ripples on a pond. "We are rolling in and out of the passing ripples. This has to be more than a super nova though. Less than a quasar or the planet would be swept of life. Less than a micro blackhole or a primal particle or we would have super volcanoes and it would only happen once. Not a passing wormhole or our sun would collapse too."

He paused and tapped his pencil. Paulo tilted his head. He looked back at his Internet connection still on the story about the super tidal wave striking Antarctica. "Three separate quakes."

His eyes widened. Dr. Restrepo returned to his paper and drew a triangle between three dots. He drew ripples out from each one and marked X's where they combined. He knew this was scratched speculation and not real numbers yet, but he was working on a theory from the moment – or the idea of a theory.

He drew one last dark curve around each dot and drew lines pulling the curves together where they would meet for one combined tidal wave.

Paulo swallowed and switched the computer to a new calculation. He needed the details of the waves that had passed already, the available data on the three stars, and an exact magnitude of the final wave. That was a lot and he suspected his time was short.

It was probably time to call the director to set up that call, but he had to be sure. If the final wave was going to be large enough to knock the Earth out of orbit or to cause the collapse of their own sun the way it had done to the previous stars, *then it would just be cruel to tell people.*

"I'll make the call, if there is hope we could survive," he said. "If ..."

12

Holden and Grant Grayson – Arkansas

Holden stared out the window at the passing countryside. They had left Little Rock a while ago and were on open road again. Grant was playing with his blocks. Every time he dropped one, Holden reached down to retrieve it and gave it back to his brother before he had time to cry much.

Uncle Carter and Mom had been laughing, sang along with the radio, and played twenty questions with Holden through Little Rock. Now they were back to talking in hushed tones. Carter had turned up the radio a little, but they weren't singing along. A report about global earthquakes had come on and Carter quickly switched to a CD. They still weren't singing along. They were quietly arguing the way that mom and dad used to do before they split.

Holden decided they were probably talking about dad. He stared out the window.

Leaves blew in the wind above the ground in a pattern that made sense and Holden sighed.

Then, he saw the stick. He sat up to get a better look. It wasn't exactly large, but it was too big to be carried by the wind. Holden squinted and watched it turn in the air.

He whispered. "Playground magic."

The stick coiled and turned around on its self. It was too flexible. As its head lashed out angrily at the air, Holden realized it was a snake floating several feet above the ground. He shivered and looked away.

Grant pointed out his window. "Look."

Crater and mom were still speaking in their secret tone and not paying attention to anything else.

Holden sat up and looked where his brother pointed. A field of cows ate grass. One turned in a circle kicking its feet a few inches off the ground. If they hadn't been looking right at it, the boys probably would have missed it the way the adults seemed to.

Another cow jumped and bobbed higher in the air.

Grant laughed and touched the window as he pointed. The spit from his finger being in his mouth smeared the glass over Holden's view of the flying cow. Grant said, "Over the Moon."

Holden nodded, but stared in silence.

"Don't smear Carter's windows, Baby," Mom said.

Holden looked forward to see if she saw it. She was back to talking with Carter. She saw the glass, but not the flying cow outside it.

Grant dropped another block and it floated through the air to Holden's side of the car. Grant stretched his arm out toward his older brother. "Hey. Mine."

Holden flicked the block with one finger and it sailed back to Grant's side. Grant caught it. "Got it. Hey, Mom. Watch what we can do."

"Not right now, Honey. The adults are talking. Don't interrupt."

Grant stuck out his bottom lip and released the block again. It floated out a few inches, but then dropped like normal to the floorboard again.

Grant let out a long, shrill whine and reached for the floor as far as he could from his car seat. Holden leaned down and picked up the block before handing it back to Grant.

Grant stared at the block and back at his brother. "Over the Moon?"

Holden shook his head and put a finger over his lips.

13

Michael Strove and Roman Nikitin – Russia

Michael moved back from the mouth of the cave farther back on the damp, muddy floor in the dark. The opening was covered, but not enough and the search parties were getting closer. Their pattern was meticulous and he couldn't imagine them missing the hiding spot once they got close enough. If he tried to flee now though, they would be on him for sure.

Michael had tried to sleep, but couldn't stay out for more than a few minutes at a time. Pain and stress were robbing him of the ability and he knew it would catch up with him soon and at the worst moment.

Roman's eyes were open across from him.

Michael fished out a protein bar from his pocket and broke it in half. Roman accepted the half he was offered. "Yum. The breakfast of an American champion, no?"

Michael took a bite and unlatched the canteen from his belt. "You need to stay off the Internet, Roman."

"I have for years now," he said between bites.

Michael nodded. "So your family got you into this trouble?"

Roman shrugged. "Not so bad a place until the invisible tiger started crushing towers with me inside."

Michael smiled. "It would be a beautiful place if the Russian army wasn't hunting me and the trees would stop falling down on us."

Michael offered Roman the canteen, but Roman waved him off. Michael knew Roman needed to drink, but he did not have the energy to try to force him, so Michael just took another swallow for himself.

Roman said, "You know family names are new in Russia?"

Michael narrowed his eyes. He thought this was the opening for a joke, but Roman wasn't smiling. Michael said, "You didn't used to have a last name?"

"Less than a hundred years," Roman said. "Most families made them up during the census after the czars and the communists. Russia needed them to track the people, so we made them. If not for the census, I would just be another Roman with no family name to be punished for. Most Russian names mean 'belongs to.' So, we all belong to someone and all the trouble that family brings."

Michael nodded. "I guess that is true of all families."

"Does Captain Michael and Brother Carter come with trouble?"

"Sometimes." Michael smiled. "Our father was a religious man, a part time preacher."

"He would have liked my mother, no?"

Michael nodded. "Probably. It was a strict house. Lots of demands. Carter and I spent a lot of time trying to do better than the other so that our dad would ride the other about doing better. It made us competitive for our parents' approval."

"That is how most brothers work, I think." Roman smiled and finished his power bar.

"I love him, but we both cast shadows that make life hard for the other one. It made things tense sometimes. It made it hard for people outside our families to love us, I think. Neither of us is married or has kids. I think that made our parents sad while they were still around. Just another time we disappointed them. We spend a lot of our lives chasing something, but what exactly, I don't know."

Roman pointed at the entrance of the cave. "Now you are being chased."

"True."

"So Captain Michael becomes US Airforce fighter pilot and Brother Carter becomes American hero firefighter and that is not good enough for either one of you to think you made it?"

"That about sums is up, Roman."

Roman nodded. "I'm in exile for my mother's dreams of a better Russia. You and Brother Carter exile yourselves when you already live in an awesome democracy."

"It sounds bad when you say it like that."

Roman laughed. "Don't pay attention to me. I learned all my English from movies on the Internet."

An explosion outside vibrated the ground under them. They looked at each other and crawled to the mouth of the cave together. Smoke rose up, but then raced back down and crawled along the ground. Soldiers collapsed and lay on their bellies about a quarter mile away.

"We need to go for the station now," Roman said.

"The sun is still up," Michael said.

Roman pointed. "The invisible tiger is over there, but not here. We need to move now while they are held down."

"The gravity might travel over us here. It has happened the other times."

"It might not," Roman said. "We should go now. Trust me."

Michael looked at Roman and nodded. He looped Roman's arm over his shoulder and they limped out of the cover of the cave together.

Dr. Paulo Restrepo – Colombia

He held his cellphone out at arm's length so he could see it as the woman dabbed make-up on his cheeks. "I'm announcing a global disaster. Why does it matter if I have shine on my nose?"

She said, "You will be seen all over the world in a few minutes."

"Still doesn't answer my question."

She continued her work without responding.

The lights flared on bright and he blinked against the glare. Someone rolled a video monitor showing a star chart into Paulo's line of sight. Someone put a clicker on the arm of his chair.

He held his phone out in the light. He had a signal, but it was weak. He pulled up the number and selected it before bringing the phone to his ear.

"Jenny … no, stop talking a moment. I need to talk quickly. Are you near a television? … Yes, turn it on … Now. It doesn't matter which one … Is that firefighter boy with you … I'm not making fun. Is he? … Okay good. Stay in your house. Listen to the broadcast and do everything I tell you … I don't have time to explain now … Do you have it on? … Jenny? Jenny, are you there?"

He held the phone out and cursed. Paulo scrolled to the number again. Someone took the phone from his hand and disappeared out of the light. The make-up artist vanished too. Someone put the clicker in his hand.

A voice from out of the darkness said, "You'll be able to hear the others through your earpiece. The red light will come on in a moment. Do not start until we say though. The others will talk first. I'll count you in and point when you are to begin. Okay?"

Paulo nodded and looked at the star chart on his screen. Green spots danced in his vision from the bright studio lights. He could not remember what he was supposed to say.

He looked back forward and the red light was on. He took a deep breath and got ready to speak. Then, he remembered they were going to count him in and point. He couldn't see though. He wondered if he had missed the signal. He stared forward without saying anything.

Sean Grayson and Jenny Restrepo – West Memphis, Arkansas

Jenny scrolled through her contacts and tried more than one, but she was getting no signal on calls or data. "Is your phone working, Sean?"

"I have power." Sean turned the phone where it sat on the side table. "I'm getting no signal though. Did your father say what channel?"

"No. He sounded frantic though. I'm scared, Sean."

Sean stopped flipping channels. "Looks like it doesn't matter."

"Why?" Jenny set down her phone.

"The same broadcast is on every one." Sean leaned forward and pointed with the remote. "Isn't that your father?"

"Where?" Jenny sat down next to him.

He waved the remote. "On the split screen. On the left."

"Turn it up."

"It is up."

"Turn it up more and stop talking."

Sean looked at her, but did what she said.

The screen switched to the group of men in suits and lab coats and Jenny's dad vanished from view. Camera bulbs flashed and the man held up a hand as he began to speak. "It is vital that the following information be given out to the world, so no interruptions or questions, please, until we have said everything that needs to be said."

Sean swallowed and glanced at Jenny. She was wringing her hands and sitting out on the edge of the sofa.

Sean switched hands for the remote and put a hand on her shoulder. "Is this what your father was trying to tell us about before the cellphone cut out?"

"I don't know. Let's listen."

The man on the screen continued. "Strange phenomenon involving fluctuations in gravity, normally considered a constant, have been experienced at various parts of the world. A few astronomers have noticed anomalies in the appearance of the stars due to these gravitational waves. Due to the regularity of the gravitational waves traveling through our solar system, the revolution of the Earth has taken us between these waves of distortion. As the Earth's path encounters one, it travels through our planet. Movement in the Earth's core and shifting in tectonic plates has caused seismic events of various intensities. It has also changed our perception of gravity within the sometimes narrow path of the waves. With a few exceptions, the Eastern Hemisphere has experienced the entering waves as heavier gravity. The Western Hemisphere has experienced the exiting waves as lighter than normal gravity."

Reporters began shouting questions and the man waved his hands calling for them to quiet.

Jenny whispered. "This is crazy."

"I saw it," Sean said.

"What? When?"

"During the fire," Sean licked his lips and closed his eyes. "Objects were floating in the building. I lifted a beam off that boy because it weighed nothing in that moment. I floated with him up the hallway like we were weightless in space. Then, gravity came back and it all crashed down."

She rubbed his back. "Why didn't you say something? That was a couple days ago. Have you been holding this all in?"

"I didn't think I could be believed. Admitting hallucinations is not the best move in my line of work or with my ... history."

Jenny hugged him. "It was all real. You could have told me. You can tell me anything."

"I know. I was scared."

The man on television said, "Please, everyone quiet. Time is short. Einstein had predicted that exploding stars would create gravitational distortions in spacetime. This theory was proven years ago by LIGO, a gravitational wave detection laboratory.

The recent strange phenomena we have seen around the globe were created by strong gravitational waves. These waves were created by the collapse of Alpha Centauri, one of our closest neighbors in the galactic neighborhood. This collapse occurred some time ago and its waves were periodically going toward our sun and earth sometimes crossed its path. One physicist and astronomer, Dr. Paulo Restrepo of the Marlo-Pitts observatory in South America, was able to quantify the effect and clue the rest of the scientific community in on it. What he discovered though was that the collapse of Alpha Centauri was actually the third in a cascade of three stars. The net effect of that triple collapse and the last cumulative wave pulse will pass through the Earth in a few hours from now."

"Some global satellites have been knocked out of orbit by the waves so far and very likely there will be many more lost soon, so we need to get all of this information out as quickly as possible. Please, listen closely."

"It will again enter through the Eastern Hemisphere and exit through the West, but the effect will be far more intense. People in the Eastern Hemisphere should stay low to the ground away from water, hard surfaces, stay outside of vehicles of any kind, and away from loose structures or other objects that might fall. The G forces will be intense and may result in unconsciousness or injury. Do not hold other people under you during the effect. This includes adults or children."

"In the Western Hemisphere, the effect will be more than weightlessness experienced by some in the path of previous waves. People should be inside stable structures. Remove all loose objects including heavy furniture. Tie down to something solid if possible to limit injury. Objects as large as cars may be lifted high in the atmosphere. Some objects may actually leave Earth's atmosphere or come crashing back down from a great height. You must get inside now and prepare. There will still be danger from falling debris after the wave has passed."

"Governments all over the world are now grounding flights, preparing shelters, and clearing highways. Do not delay. Do not try to travel to relatives that are not in your immediate area as this will just put you and them at risk."

"Lastly, Dr. Restrepo has done meticulous calculations. I and others have carefully checked his work. We are confident in the information we have just told you and world governments are acting on it for your safety as we speak. Dr. Restrepo also believes that while this event will have devastating surface effects as I have just described to you, he assures us that the Earth's core, Earth's orbit, and our own sun will be spared from the destruction that overtook less stable stars that sent these waves in our direction."

"We as a planet and as a global community will survive. We will rebuild. Please, follow my instructions and the instructions of your local authorities so that you will be a part of that rebuilding."

"Dr. Restrepo will now share his findings from the Marlo-Pitts Observatory in Colombia before we take questions."

The screen shifted and Jenny's father stared into the camera on a split screen with a star chart. "I will make this simple so that it is easy to understand and the facts are before you. You will see Alpha Centauri here in proximity of our solar system. The other two stars in question are ..."

The screen went blue.

Jenny say up. "Turn it back on."

Sean poked at the buttons on the remote. "We have no signal. Check online. I'm sure it's streaming there."

Jenny ran and opened her laptop. "Internet is down."

She clicked on the radio on the shelf and hit search/scan. The radio sounded off a hiss of static and the digital numbers rolled through the channels over and over finding nothing.

"Everything is down," she said.

"The boys." Sean's face went pale.

"What are you talking about?"

He shook his head. "Tabitha and Carter took Holden and Grant camping. They are out there in the open. They are probably already out there."

"I'm sure they heard," Jenny said. "They'll find shelter."

"How? They are in the Ouachita National Forest. There is nothing there. They'll have their cellphones off. Even if they check now, everything is down. There is not even any radio. They won't know it's coming. They'll die."

Jenny took hold of Sean's shoulders as the static from the radio hissed in the room. "How far away are they?"

Sean swallowed. "All the way across the state. The Black Fork Mountain Wilderness is remote. There are no cars and no one is even supposed to camp up there. They are all alone."

"That is really far," she said dropping her hands. "We have less than seven hours."

"I have to try," Sean said. "They are my sons. Carter is my friend. Tabby is their mother. We have to try."

Jenny nodded and grabbed her keys. "We'll take my jeep. It has four wheel drive if we need to drive where cars aren't supposed to drive."

"I'll go," Sean said. "You stay here and stay inside like they said on TV."

She kissed him on the mouth and ran for the door. "Thank you, but not a chance. Let's go, redneck hero. We have to cross the entire state."

Sean thought he should probably gather some supplies. He wasn't sure what and he couldn't think clearly. Time was running out and his boys were in danger. He ran for the door after Jenny. They left the radio searching for a signal and hissing static at the empty house.

16

Michael Strove and Roman Nikitin – Russia

Michael charged forward between the light and shadows cut between the trees that were still standing. Roman kept a good pace for hobbling, but it wasn't as fast as he would have liked. They were passing more and more open ground with fallen, broken trees too.

A bullet tore through a tree trunk on a spot a few feet above his head and just ahead of them. Bark and central wood exploded out and peppered out around them. Michael ducked his head as they ran through. He was just glad the pieces fell at a normal rate instead of firing to the ground like sharp bullets.

They hurdled a fallen tree and then another. These looked to be old logs that had come down when nature still obeyed the old rules of gravity.

Michael stepped off into open space and couldn't find the ground. He tried to get his balance on the slope, but the two of them fell down the hill head over heels. His shoulder connected to a rock with jarring pain that quickly reminded him that he had narrowly survived a plane crash. Michael's knee wretched under his body and the captain yelped from the sickening agony. His hip slammed a log and Michael tried to claw himself to a stop on it, but raked off thinking he had pulled off one of his fingernails.

The slope became steeper and the men tumbled harder and faster.

Michael slammed to a stop staring up from his back at clouds painted with the bright colors of the setting sun.

"Roman?"

Michael tried to sit up, but winced.

Roman's face entered his line of sight and covered the colorful clouds. The Russian pulled the captain up to sitting and Michael cried out.

"Broken, Michael?"

"I don't think I can keep going, Roman. Can you get to safety before I surrender?"

"They have seen me and will keep following until they find out who I am," Roman said. "And it's not nothing that we are in this together, Michael. So, get up. We are getting closer."

Roman dragged Michael to his feet and Michael leaned more on Roman instead of the other way around. "How much closer?"

"Not as much as we would like, but we will get there. Once we are inside, we will be safe."

As they pressed forward, Michael looked back at the colors under the clouds. The brightness was dying and purple was painting over what had been there moments before.

Something about the idea of being inside bothered Michael. He could not place why. He pictured his older brother in all his gear running into a burning building and Michael sensed that same level of danger about going inside.

Michael shook his head and pulled his eyes away from the sky.

He thought about Carter and said a prayer in his mind for his brother. He had no reason to think Carter was in any danger beyond his normal job, but with the strange things going on with the rules of the world, he didn't know, so he said the prayer.

Michael looked back at the darkening sky in time to see the clouds dissolve and fall to the ground as swirling fog. He heard trees cracking to his right. Michael bowed his head and they continued forward.

17

Sean Grayson and Jenny Restrepo – Little Rock, Arkansas

Traffic crawled forward again. Sean slammed his fist into the steering wheel until the heel of his hand hurt.

"Do you want me to drive?" Jenny asked.

"We're not driving," Sean said. "We are parked."

Jenny put her hand on the back of the driver's seat of her jeep where Sean sat behind the wheel. She stopped short of putting her hand on his shoulder and Sean noticed.

Jenny said, "I can do the parking for a while until we get clear of all this."

Sean took a deep breath and smelled thick exhaust wafting around him in the open jeep. The cars stretched endlessly ahead of them across the expressway. Sean could see the exit ramp about a quarter mile ahead. Cars jammed every lane up the slope and sat clogged over the bridge of the overpass. He glanced at the shoulder on their side and over the median at opposing traffic. Cars had filled the emergency lane and the gritty edge of the road to create one more lane of congestion.

"No, I'm fine. It won't matter anyway." Sean laid his head against the steering wheel. "My kids are going to die because I can't get to them in time. I should have said something about what happened in the building and maybe things would be different. I should have fought for them and insisted that she honor my weekend. They would have all probably stayed in town and we would all be safe even if she was ticked at me for it. She's always mad at me anyway, but I just let them go. I always just let them go and that's why they are growing up without a father."

"They have a father." Jenny put her hand on his neck then. "You are doing fine. You are being a good father now regardless of what may have happened in the past. None of that can be changed now, so there is no point in destroying yourself over it."

Sean lifted his head to look across traffic with tears in his eyes. "Now they won't grow up at all. We can't get there in time. We will never make it in all of this."

Several men got out of a truck and opened the driver's door of an old, tan Buick. Sean thought there was about to be a fight, but then he saw the tan car had been abandoned and was sitting empty. Traffic had moved so little that he hadn't noticed. The men shifted the car into neutral and turned the wheel all the way to the side. They hunkered down and pushed it rolling the car sideways through the lanes between bumpers until it dove nose first into the standing water along the side of the expressway.

The men ran back to their truck and traffic rolled forward a few feet. Another blue sedan whipped over into the space the men had opened in the lane and halted progress again. The men shouted and cursed. The fellow in the blue car rolled down his window and yelled back.

Sean came to a halt behind the truck. Through a break in the hills beyond the expressway, he got a better view of the high rises that marked downtown Little Rock. Enormous swatches of glass were missing from two of them exposing openings into the offices inside. He wondered if that destruction had occurred when floating desks impacted the glass from the inside before coming crashing down with full gravity again.

How had Carter missed that? Sean shook his head. *He thought it was from the quakes. That's what any sane person would think.*

Scorch marks up the exposed framework of one of the shattered buildings caught Sean's eye. He wasn't close enough to get a good feel for whether the fire had originated from within the skyscraper or from something from the outside. He imagined a helicopter pilot suddenly navigating a weightless craft over the city only to have that weight come back again suddenly.

He hoped they were able to get all the planes down before the next and greatest wave hit like Jenny's dad had predicted. He hoped that it would matter. They said people would be safe inside buildings, but could they really know? Looking at the large buildings of downtown Little Rock, he questioned whether inside was safe at all. Would they stand up to the pressures of being yanked upward and back down again. Even if the sun and Earth survived, would this be the end of people?

Sean thought about Carter's brother Michael. He was in the Airforce and posted overseas. Sean couldn't remember where. Carter and Sean had not made much small talk recently. He wondered if Michael was in the crush zone or the float zone of all of this. He hoped he wasn't in the air during any of it. Sean thought a little prayer for his sons and for Michael.

Michael would want me to save Carter. I need to get to my sons and save all of them. I have to.

The men got out of their truck again. Sean watched and expected them to shove another abandoned vehicle off the road. They opened the door to the blue car and dragged the driver out. People on both sides were yelling and honking.

Sean cursed.

Jenny shook her head and covered her mouth. "What are they doing? We need to stop this."

The driver took the first swing and then the men were on him. He was curled on the ground against his front tire as the men kicked and beat him.

"Sean?"

"There's nothing I can do, Jenny."

"Why are people acting like this?"

A gunshot rang off and one of the men fell. Others ran and dove behind cars. Another shot was fired and the windshield of the blue car exploded into shards.

Sean turned the wheel of the jeep and drove across. He scraped the passenger's side of the vehicle across someone's front bumper. Glass from a headlight lamp blasted up into the air behind them

"Sean, what're you doing?"

"Getting us out of here."

He drove through another gap just before the pick-up truck backed into the car behind it, crumpling the hood of a car and blaring the horn of the smashed car in one, endless note.

Sean dragged along the back bumper of an SUV on his side of the jeep throwing sparks up around his leg. One more gap and he would be over the shoulder and off the highway. From there, he had no idea what to do next.

One of the men that had been kicking a man on the ground a moment ago grabbed hold of the open jamb of the door on Sean's driver's side of the jeep. The man brought one boot up onto the running board and the other dragged the pavement under the jeep. He grabbed Sean's sleeve. "Get out or I'll throw you both out on your heads."

Sean stepped down on the accelerator while lifting his left foot as high as he could in the seat. He extended his knee connecting with the man's chin with his heel. The man's hands came loose and he folded backward in the air from the kick. The fellow landed on his back sprawled across the trunk of a Honda. The man rose up on his elbows and shook his head like he had just woken up from a bad dream.

Sean left the highway in the air before he let off the gas. The jeep bounced twice going down the small slope. It tilted hard to one side and then the other with each impact threatening to topple with the high center of gravity of the jeep.

Very high center of gravity if we are still in it when that wave passes through the Earth, Sean thought despite the desperate situation around him.

It splashed down in the soggy grass off the highway and slogged forward with sluggish weight. Sean stepped down on the gas again spinning black water and muck up into the air behind them. He thought about the mob and the attacker behind him, but he did not turn to look.

"A little less gravity might be good about now," Sean said as he shifted gears and pumped the gas.

"What?" Jenny looked around them as specks of mud landed on the dash and their seats.

The wheels caught and lurched forward before bogging down again. He prepared to shift again, but the jeep tilted up in the front and bounded forward off the wet ground. Dry grass tore under the tires and sprayed out in their wake on both sides.

Before Sean could make a decision about where to go next, he swerved around a small tree only to plow through and over a low, wire fence. Metal raked and tore under the jeep as it spun out into a grassy pasture. Sean turned out of the fishtail and ripped the jeep up over the rolling hills.

As they topped one knoll, they saw a pond and a herd of cattle staring dumbly up at the passing jeep. Sean spotted a gate farther along on the opposing fence. He steered around logs and missed a couple trenches by inches.

Sean centered on the gate and raced toward it.

"Lock." Jenny shouted.

"What?"

"The gate is padlocked, Sean. Look."

He nodded. "Hang on. Sorry, I can't afford to stop. We're running out of time."

Sean picked up speed and squinted his eyes. The front of the jeep slammed the gate head on with enough force to hurt his teeth. As the gate flung open with the force of the impact, Sean saw that the lock and chain had held, but the post had torn loose from the ground flying through the air pulled by the chain.

He thought about every object on the planet being flung up in the air and Sean pressed the pedal down harder. He found a dirt road and turned onto it flinging dust and rocks in a cloud behind them.

Sean shook his head and said, "Sorry about that."

"Not as sorry as the farmer will be when his cows get away."

Sean shrugged. "If your father is right about all of this, they may be flying away."

"He's right. He's always right," Jenny said.

Sean cut a glance at her face seeing the deep set concern as the wind whipped strands of hair around her cheeks. The look of concern was not directed at him this time, but it bothered him and scared him more than all the looks of concern he had endured over the years. He looked back forward.

Ahead he saw a paved road and no farmers had shot at him. *I haven't been shot at for almost a full minute.*

They bounded up onto the road with no lines dividing one lane from the other. Sean drove on the wrong side as he looked at the sky to see which way west was. He seemed to be headed mostly west. The sky was crystal clear blue. Normally that was the perfect day in his book, but he also knew it meant high pressure. He wondered if the comings and goings of gravity were impacting atmospheric pressure. Sean thought lower gravity would mean less pressure, but he didn't know. *It's not really lower gravity, but gravity moving the wrong direction.*

Sean turned his attention back on the road and steered onto the correct side of the street.

"Sean?"

He saw the fire belching out from the crumpled hood of a station wagon crashed into a telephone pole on the side of the road. "I see it."

He swerved out wide around it. Jenny looked at him and back at the car. A woman spilled out of the driver's side and pulled at the back door without budging it. Sean saw a girl beating on the inside of the glass and another in a car seat reaching for her mom.

The jeep raced past.

"Sean, the kids."

"I saw. Hold on."

He swerved to the side and ran up over a curb onto the grass next to a parking lot. Sean jumped out and Jenny started to follow. He grabbed her arm. "No, stay with the Jeep. If we leave it, someone may try to steal it and we'll be stranded. If there is trouble, honk."

"Okay. Hurry. The car is on fire and those kids are inside."

He grabbed a fire extinguisher out of the back of the jeep and ran. Sean sprayed inside the engine under the openings in the bent hood. The fire fell back and white smoke billowed out. As the extinguisher sputtered empty, the fire blasted back out again.

He moved the mother aside and shouted. "Move away from the glass. Cover your sister's eyes."

The girl turned away and put her hand over her sister's eyes. Sean was impressed. The girl had to be younger than Holden and she was good under pressure.

Sean swung and shattered the side window with one strike. The mother screamed. Sean swept glass out of the window frame with the body of the extinguisher before he tossed it aside.

"Come on." He held his hands inside.

The girl unbuckled her sister and walked her across the seat to Sean. He pulled the girl out and handed her off to the mother. *You should be a firefighter. You have the iron for it, girl.*

Fire and smoke swallowed the front of the car and licked along the sides. He reached back in. "Come on. Hurry."

Sean took her under his arm like a sack and guided the mother toward the jeep. Flame wrapped over the car and one of the windows shattered behind them.

He set the girl down on the grass and the mother hugged them both. Seeing it made Sean feel farther from his boys than before.

A man approached from the direction of the store attached to the parking lot. Sean looked at Jenny in the jeep and then stepped between the man and the mother and her girls.

The man said, "I can try to call someone, but I don't think anyone will come. The whole city has gone insane."

"Did you hear the news?" Sean asked.

"The gravity thing?" The man nodded. "Yes, we're inside locking everything down so the place doesn't fly apart around us."

"Can they go inside with you until it's over?" Sean waved back at the family behind him.

"Yes, of course, what about you?"

"I'm trying to get to my sons. I have to go."

The man nodded. "Good luck to you."

Sean turned and ran without waiting for thanks from the family. He jumped into the jeep and hooked back around onto the road. As he looked to be sure no cars were coming, he saw the older sister waving. The mother and the store owner were walking the girls toward the store.

Sean waved back and raced away.

"You did the right thing," Jenny said.

"I know."

"We'll still make it. Everything will be fine," she said.

Sean swallowed, but did not speak.

Jenny rubbed the back of his neck with one hand as he drove and Sean started to cry.

"It will be fine," she said again. "I'm always right."

Sean sniffed and nodded. "Yeah, we haven't been shot at for minutes and I haven't been almost burned to death for seconds. We are having a great day."

"You left my fire extinguisher back there," she said. "You're the one that made me get it."

He nodded. "When that wave hits, it will just lift up in the air and fall back on our heads. We're better off without it right now."

He glanced back at the clear sky and kept driving.

18

Holden Grayson, Grant Grayson, and Carter Strove – Ouachita
National Forest, Black Fork Mountain Wilderness, Arkansas

Holden picked up another rock and skipped it over the lake from
the end of the dock. They had to hike in from where they parked the car
and they didn't have a boat. *What's the point of a dock with no boat? I
wish my dad was here. It would be better with Dad.*

Grant handed him another rock. Holden held it up and shook his
head. "No, it has to be flat and smooth."

Grant dug through the pile of stones they had carried with them to
the end of the dock. Grant traded Holden a flat one for the fat, round
stone. "This one?"

Holden held it up above his head like he was inspecting it in the sun
against the blue sky. "It will do."

"Can you get it all the way to the other side, Holden?"

Holden laughed. "No, that's like a mile away."

He flung the rock side arm and it skipped five times before
plunging below the water.

"What if you use magic?" Grant asked.

"There's no such thing." Holden blinked against a burn behind his
eyes. He did not know why he felt like crying, but he just did
sometimes.

"Yeah, there is. You did it in the car with the block. Remember?"

Holden looked back and saw Carter on his hands and knees blowing
at some smoky leaves in a circle of rocks. Holden shook his head. "I
don't know what happened in the car, Grant."

"And with the cows. Like that."

"I wasn't doing that. It just happened."

Grant shrugged. "Okay. Throw more rocks, Holden."

"You do one, Grant."

"I can't. I'm all little still."

"Try. No one will see, but me."

Grant held the fat, round rock up above his head and looked at it the
way he had seen Holden do. He brought it down and drew his arm back
behind his back.

Holden shook his head. "You need a flat one."

Grant threw it anyway. The stone hurled in an arc before plopping down into the water with a high splash.

"I did it, Holden."

Holden shook his head. "You need to use one of the flat stones."

The round rock rose up out of the water and hovered just about the surface. It was dark from being wet. A fish with a spotted back jumped out and bit at it in the air. The rock bounded off the fish's lips. The rock tumbled in the air bouncing slowly off the surface of the water five, seven, fourteen times until Holden couldn't see it anymore.

"All the way across the lake. See?" Grant said.

The fish whipped its tail as if trying to fling itself back in the water. It twisted in a circle just above and opened its mouth over and over. Holden thought about fish flopping in a boat as they died in the air. *This is what it would look like with no boat*, he thought.

The fish touched the water again with its side. It flapped in a wild panic splashing water up into the air around it.

Grant laughed.

The fish caught enough traction to pull itself back under. The weight of the water seemed to be enough to keep it under this time.

Carter said from behind them. "Come for a walk with me, boys."

Holden gasped and stumbled forward with his toes just inches from the edge of the dock. *Would I go under or float above it in the air? I don't know how things work anymore.*

Grant kicked at the rocks scattering them across the end of the dock. A half dozen tipped over the edge and dropped into the lake. Ripples spread out from the impacts driving out rings that disrupted their inverted reflections staring up at them as they stared down. The ripples crossed one another slicing patterns that were harder to follow with the eye. Out from the center they seemed to combine in a more powerful ripple which traveled out from them and was gone like Grant's magic rock skipping slowly away leaving them forever.

"Did you see my rock go?" Grant asked.

Carter said, "No, buddy, I missed it."

"It went forever. All the way across the lake. Tell him, Holden."

Holden stared down into the water not saying anything.

"Wow, all the way across," Carter said. "That's amazing."

"It was amazing," Grant said.

Holden recognized the tone in Carter's voice that adults took when they humored a kid, but did not believe what they were saying. Grant didn't hear it and thought Carter really thought Grant's throw was amazing instead of unbelievable.

Grant pointed out toward the center of the lake. "Did you see the fish?"

"I missed that too," Carter said.

"It was flying in the air like the flying cows." Grant dropped his hand.

"Amazing," Carter said.

Holden took a deep breath. "Yeah, amazing."

"Let's take that walk. I need to talk to you boys about some stuff."

The boys turned and walked beside Carter off the dock and past the campsite.

"We're going for a walk with Uncle Carter, Mom," Grant said.

"I know," she said. "I'll see you all in a minute."

They walked up the hill into the trees. Holden thought about the story of Hansel and Gretel being led out into the woods by the witch's house because the step mom didn't want to feed them anymore.

"Look at those big rocks," Grant said.

The outcropping rose above them. Deep slices ringed the sides horizontally. The stratified sections made the formation look like they were stacked on each other in layers instead of being one solid rock.

"Those are big, buddy," Carter said.

"Where are we going?" Holden asked.

"Here is as good a place as any," Carter said.

Holden remembered that the woodcutter was sent to finish the kids off in the woods, but disobeyed the mother by letting them live. *I forgot to drop breadcrumbs on the way up here from the car*, Holden thought. *The birds would just eat them anyway. I should have used stones.*

"Can we climb them?" Grant asked.

"Maybe in a minute," Carter said as he sat on the lip of one of the bottom folds of the rock. "I need to talk to you two about something."

"Are there caves?" Grant asked standing on the rock looking straight up the side next to where Carter sat.

"Maybe. We'd have to look. We have to be careful though because snakes will get into the shadows of these rocks to hide and stay warm. We need to watch where we step and where we put our hands."

"What did you need to talk about?" Holden asked.

Carter stared at him a moment, he laughed, and looked away. "Yeah, ugh, well, you guys know your daddy and I are friends, right?"

"You fight fires together," Grant said still staring up.

"Right. And I like your mother a lot," Carter said. "I love her. Even though that is true, I'm not trying to replace your daddy. He will always be your daddy and I will always be his friend. Do you guys understand what I am saying?"

"Do the snakes jump out?" Grant asked.

"What?" Carter shook his head. "No, they won't. We'll be fine."

Holden thought about the snake twisting the air on their way up to the campground and he shivered.

"What do they eat?" Grant asked.

Carter smiled. "Like mice and voles and stuff. They eat things that need to be eaten. The snakes get a bad rap. They'll leave us alone, if we are careful. Listen, what I wanted to talk to you boys about is that I'm going to ask your mommy to marry me and I wanted you guys to know about it before that happened."

"Are you going to come live with us?" Grant asked.

"We are talking about all that, but, yeah, that's what would happen then."

"You would stay in mommy's room or get your own room?" Grant asked.

"Ugh, well, see. We'd be married so ..."

"You shouldn't have told Grant," Holden said. "He can't keep a secret."

Carter laughed. "That's okay. Your mother knows it's coming. I just need to do the actual, official ask is all. I think that will be this weekend on this trip."

"Did you get a ring?" Holden asked.

"Here in my pocket. You want to see it?"

"Mommy already has rings," Grant said. "You should get her something else like a crown or maybe a horse."

Carter laughed and ran his hand over the top of Grant's head. "I'll treat her like a princess though."

Holden rolled his eyes.

"The crown and horse would help," Grant said. "Does Dad know yet?"

Carter swallowed and looked away. "Not yet. We'll get around to that."

"Daddy used to be married to Mommy too," Grant said, "but not anymore. Did you know about all that, Uncle Carter?"

Carter nodded. "Yeah, that came up."

"Some of the kids at school say stuff about you being friends with Mommy," Grant said.

"What kind of stuff?" Carter asked.

"Don't talk about that," Holden said.

"No, it's okay," Carter said.

"Mom told Grant not to talk about it," Holden said.

"What kind of stuff are we talking about, Holden?"

Holden shrugged. "Some of the kids' parents don't like black people. Mom says they repeat stuff they hear their parents say. We aren't supposed to repeat it."

Carter nodded. "We can talk about all that later some time."

Grant pointed up. "Holden, do you think this rock can fly like the other stuff from the magic? Do you think? It would hurt, if it fell on us."

Holden turned away and looked back in the direction of the campsite where they had left their mom. He didn't want to be out there anymore.

19

Michael Strove and Roman Nikitin – Russia

They were moving from tree to tree. Michael left one trunk and reached out to brace his weight on the next one. The trees were getting further apart and fewer of them were standing as cover grew thin.

Michael did not trust the darkness to protect them either. Search lights from the jeeps on the road running parallel to their path swept through the scant woods around them. That suggested that they weren't relying on night vision, but it seemed scant comfort at best.

Michael wasn't sure who was supporting who any longer as he and Roman wobbled forward through the darkness in the wilderness.

Roman stopped and pulled Michael back the other direction. "Wait."

"What is it? Do you hear something?"

"Need to find the way."

Michael bowed his head and heaved for air. "You said we were close."

"We are. It just feels far because we are hurt and the Russian army is chasing us."

Michael nodded his head and blinked on sweat rolling into his eyes making it even harder to see in the dark. Michael thought that Roman's statement would be quite funny under other circumstances. He imagined himself telling it to other pilots in a mess hall as a funny piece about his harrowing adventure after crashing in Russia. He realized the image felt like an unreal fantasy. Getting out alive to tell his story felt more far-fetched than the strange changes in gravity that brought him there in the first place.

As Roman oriented himself, Michael realized he could not even picture telling the story to his brother. Arkansas felt so far away in that moment. It felt farther than Alaska or an American hospital or embassy. It felt farther than the other side of the world even. A conversation with Carter about how he had survived this moment in Russia felt like something in another dimension or an alternate reality. It seemed like something that could not possibly happen in this universe.

Michael whispered. "You can't get there from here."

Roman pointed with the edge of his hand like he was chopping at the few trees that were still standing ahead of them. "No, it is this way. We are almost there. Almost. Almost. Let's go."

Michael staggered forward along the direction of Roman's chop with Roman still at his side.

Michael had resolved himself before he ever crashed over land that the mission was going to end in his death. He had prepared himself to ditch in the ocean to avoid this very thing. He hadn't had much time to contemplate life, death, gravity, or the universe in that moment, but he had mentally said his goodbyes to his brother then.

Gravity had shifted again out there over the ocean and turned his plans in another direction. He still had not allowed himself to contemplate seeing his brother again. Now the thought bothered him deeply as he still couldn't picture it, but had time to think about it.

His father had taken Carter and Grant to a conference in Atlanta back when the man was still a preacher and was giving a talk to other preachers. He couldn't remember the name of the hotel, but they had been on the fortieth floor and it was open in the middle. The balconies along the edges that lined the doors for the rooms overlooked the emptiness in the middle all the way to the lobby floor hundreds of feet down. It had been a vast abyss that left Michael feeling sick to his stomach and dizzy. He had walked close to the wall every time they approached the elevator. Carter had made fun of Michael about it. Michael had flown experimental planes at supersonic speeds near the top edge of the atmosphere, but sometimes he still had bad dreams about that empty centered hotel.

He imagined falling through the middle. The fall would have taken a few seconds and it would have ended in darkness. Michael imagined the moments of that fall. The end would come and there would be no memories, but he would think about things as the floor rushed toward him. Those thoughts would vanish in that final darkness like they had never existed even though he would have thought them. He had trouble wrapping his mind around that.

As he and Roman moved forward step by step, Michael felt like he was in the final seconds of that fall that had haunted his thoughts since he was little. He was still thinking, but the darkness would come shortly from a Russian bullet or a tree being crushed to Earth by the force Roman kept calling the invisible tiger.

It was as good a name as any for the final seconds of being pushed down by gravity into the darkness. The world did not seem real around him.

He realized he wanted to see Carter again. The thought made him feel sad and isolated.

"There." Roman pointed with a chop again.

Up the open slope, he saw the fence and a colorless metal building. A clothes line ran from one corner out to the tower of the transmitter. That did not strike Michael as promising for getting a message out or for this ending in anything but that final darkness. *A listening station with no one to listen*, he thought.

"I think gravity is going to win this time, Roman."

He laughed on Michael's shoulder. "It usually does, but you fly planes for the American heroes, right?"

"What does that have to do with anything?"

"You beat gravity all the time even though you should know better. Let's try one more time."

Michael took a deep breath and nodded.

20

Sean Grayson and Jenny Restrepo – Arkansas

Sean whipped around the side of the roadblock and cut a dark tire track through the dirt on the side. The jeep bucked as he ran back up onto the road. He raced forward as the lights and siren of one patrol vehicle pursued behind him.

"Sean, that's the police. You need to stop."

He looked in the mirror and saw the other officers standing near the roadblock. He saw a cinderblock building close to the right of the roadblock with the metal door hanging open. He turned his eyes back forward.

"We'll be fine, Jenny. Trust me."

She looked back and spoke to Sean over the siren. "The police are chasing us. Stop and tell them why we need to go. He'll understand."

"He won't, but it doesn't matter."

"You're scaring me, Sean."

Sean felt his chest growing tight. This felt familiar. He had never run from the cops before. He had never been arrested either. He had been living his life like he was running away before and he knew the fear he had put in people during those times. He heard that fear in Jenny's voice then over the pursuing siren.

"We need to get to the boys. I know what I'm doing."

"Explain it to me then," Jenny said. "Trust me enough to tell me what you think will happen here."

"He'll stop chasing us soon," Sean said.

Jenny looked back at the police car and then at Sean. "He won't. Police chase until they catch. You can't get away, Sean. Just talk to him while we still have a chance."

Sean shook his head. "He'll give up this time and soon. I know it."

"How do you know?"

The siren cut off and the police car made a U turn in the street. Jenny stared as Sean let off the gas a little, but not much.

"We're fine. We'll make it," he said. "You said so. Right?"

"How did you know he would turn around like that?"

"The gravity wave is coming. They don't want to be out here anymore than we do. He's going back to where they are going to hide when this hits."

Jenny nodded. "Brilliant."

Sean licked his lips. He did not feel brilliant. He thought about the mother and the two girls back at the store. He wondered if those were the last people he got to save. Maybe that was his last victory and time was not going to allow him another win.

Sean weaved through neighborhoods and shopping centers. Cars sat with doors hanging open. No one was outside and there were no other cars on the road. Everyone had taken the safe choice.

Sean looked to the right side of the road. He wanted to barrel forward, but he didn't want to miss the turn.

"Do you know exactly where they are?" Jenny asked.

Sean squinted as he looked out Jenny's side of the jeep. "The turn is up here. I went with Carter out here on survival training. He came out here a lot on his own over the years."

"Is it big?"

"Very big," Sean said.

"How will we find them?"

He swallowed. "There is a lake. I'm betting they are out there. Hoping."

Sean made the turn and raced up a dirt road. A drop off on one side hung very close to the wheels, but Sean couldn't bring himself to slow down.

He swerved just in time to dodge a sign that warned there was no camping and to stay on the trail.

Sean shifted into a lower gear and had to slow as the jeep climbed the rocky slope of the trail. A pine tree scraped the driver's side of the jeep. The glass from the side mirror popped loose and spun into the air off the trail behind him. Seeing it fall made him feel better. He did not understand why at first, but then Sean realized he had half expected the broken mirror to stay in the air spinning forever and ever like the balloon cup had tried to do in the smoke. If that had happened, it might have meant he was too late. *Close, but no dice, Sean*, he thought to himself. But there was still time apparently. It did not mean they were going to make it, but there was still some time at least.

The jeep bottomed out as they went down the back slope. They splashed through a low creek in a muddy slosh before climbing again.

Sean narrowed his eyes. The jeep was struggling and Carter had been driving his hatchback. He had trouble picturing Carter making this trail in that little car. If he hadn't parked back in the last parking area, maybe Sean had come to the wrong spot. There was no time to backtrack, if he had guessed wrong. This was their one shot.

Sean made the next curve and spotted Carter's hatchback. His heart leaped, but he knew they were still far away from success.

"Is that them?" Jenny asked.

Sean drove wide around the side. "That's where they parked."

He swerved back over to avoid the sign that said there were no vehicles allowed past this point. He shifted to an even lower gear and climbed the sides of smooth rocks looming large in the path as they bounded up one painful yard after another.

Sean lifted the jeep high on the passenger's side as they threaded between two boulders. He knew they were going to tip, but then the undercarriage scraped hard and the vehicle jammed to a stop. He shifted up and down spinning the wheels like he had done in the mud off the highway. The axels made harsh grinding noises as opposed to wet sprays of mud. The jeep did not budge either way.

"We have to run it, Sean."

They got out and jogged up between the rocks fighting their way up the trail. Sean started grabbing the thin pines along the trail to keep his footing and to pull himself forward. He was fit from training, but had been involved in multiple fires over the last few days without much sleep. The weariness started to set into his muscle where they met the bone.

For her part, Jenny kept a strong pace which encouraged him forward.

With the addition of fear and despair, Sean's feet felt heavy and his legs burned under him. He thought of his sons' faces and he redoubled his run. He felt heavier, but he was determined to drive forward. If he was still alive, then there was still time and he could not afford to give in to exhaustion. Holden's and Grant's lives depended on him reaching them. He had let them down too often before to let this moment be the last and final failure.

Sean stumbled and struck his cheek on a rock. His head spun and he saw blood pasted on the side as he raised his face again. Jenny took hold of his shoulders and pulled him upward. He staggered to his feet and ran forward again. He heard her footfalls behind him, but did not look back as they ran forward together.

He topped the hill and Jenny ran up to his side. Spots danced in his vision giving the world a feel of surreal abstraction. Sean heaved for breath as he looked out across the lake. There was the dock, but no car. They weren't here. *No*, he thought, *they parked back at the last clearing before I got the jeep stuck. There is no car up here. They are out there without the car. Look again, stupid.*

Sean looked down and saw the tent. There was gray smoke crawling up from a tendril off a dosed fire. Someone was here.

He spotted Holden and then Grant. Carter was standing between them, but facing away. Tabby was sitting on a folding, camping chair near the tent. They weren't looking his way, but they were there.

He still hadn't reached them. And when he did, he still had to convince them that he was telling the truth about the danger. Then, he had to figure out a way to save them. There was no time for all of that, but he had to try.

Sean started to run again.

21

Michael Strove and Roman Nikitin -- Russia

It was getting dark. The final stretch of hill opened up to a grassy slope between them and the flat gray wall on the listening station. Even though it was dark, Michael still didn't like the idea of running in the open. The tanks rolled along behind them plowing down medium-sized trees in their paths. With so many patches of forest brought down from the strange gravitational effect, Michael was surprised that there was much left in their path.

To their right a few miles in the distance to the north, jeeps looped around a logging trail between stumps of trees cut down by the hands of man and collapsed timber from the forces of the universe sweeping over Earth from some unknown force and source.

Michael heard gunfire, but could not place the direction and did not see where the shots hit.

"You need to let me go, Michael," Roman heaved for breath as he leaned on Michael's shoulder. "You can make it to the station without me pulling you down."

"Don't be silly, Roman. I wouldn't have made it this far without you helping me along. We'll make it together."

"You're going to get us both shot, Mister Hero Man."

"Will they pass you by, if I let you go?"

Roman shook his head. "You mean not shoot me for helping you? No, I think that ship has flown the chicken coop."

"Then, we get there together, Roman."

"Okay, your funeral, man."

They topped the hill and Michael stopped short of the break in the fence. He looked through at the station and then up at the sky.

Roman slid off Michael's shoulder and dropped to his knees. "What's wrong?"

"Can those tanks hit the station from there, Roman?"

Roman looked back over his shoulder and the tanks weaved between the larger trees. "Not yet, but soon."

"If we go inside, they'll fill it full of bullets and blast us with the tanks' big guns."

Roman nodded. "We stay out here and they probably still use the bullets, Michael."

"There's no message I can send out that gets me rescued in the heart of Russia before they kill me, if at all. If we go in, they will either blow the place up around us or another of those gravity waves will crush it around us like what happened to you in the tower."

"So we keep running?" Roman held out his hands.

"I think I need to surrender."

"I don't like that much, Michael."

"I'll tell them that I took you and forced you to help me, but you convinced me to give up."

Roman sighed. "Aside from not being true, they will not believe you, but I'll go along with your story if ..."

Roman noticed a falling star crossing the sky. If Roman had looked at it with a telescope he would have seen the International Space Station breaking up into small pieces as it entered the atmosphere.

Michael turned and looked at Roman when he stopped talking. Roman was still staring at the night sky and whispered. "Look at the stars."

Michael looked up. Many stars were dancing sideways, up and down as if their lights were being distorted by an invisible, fast growing gelatinous circular substance that was rapidly taking over the dark skies. A star in the center of the anomaly was getting brighter every second, illuminating the forest around them.

Roman clutched his stomach and folded to the ground. Michael felt the weight too and laid down. The pressure hit his back harder than any of the times before. He groaned in pain and then couldn't fill his lungs back again.

The remaining fence around the station crumpled flat. The station itself folded inward and crunched flat. Every tree Michael could see bent and snapped to the ground leaving only sky. A couple trees shattered spraying bark out which instantly fired toward the ground like hundreds of sharp bullets.

Michael heard explosions and screaming behind him.

Their bodies pressed into the ground cutting pits into the loose soil. As he blacked out, Michael thought, *We can't survive this one. We can't survive this one. We can't.*

22

Sean Grayson and Carter Strove – Black Fork Mountain Wilderness, Arkansas

Sean's lungs and legs were on fire as he charged down through the tangles toward the lake. The thorns tore at his skin, but he continued to run toward his sons. Jenny was right by his side.

He saw Holden point up at him. Holden was always the observant one. He saw everything first and early. Carter stood up and walked away from the shore. He squared himself between Sean and Tabitha. The boys took a couple steps toward Sean, but Tabby held them back.

He wasn't even mad. He was terrified.

"Sean?" Carter yelled. "What do you think you're doing?"

"We're in danger," Sean coughed over the phlegm built up in his throat. "We have to get to shelter now. Something is coming."

Carter held up his hands. "You need help."

Sean stopped short and dropped to his knees. Holden tried again to reach him, but Tabby pulled him back. She yelled. "Just leave us alone."

"Trust me." Sean held up his hands. "I did not race across the state to ruin your vacation. There are waves passing through the Earth from a star collapse. The next one is big – very big. It will crush things on the other side of the world and anything not tied down or inside will be blasted off the ground either out into space or to fall back like being dropped from a plane."

Carter shook his head. "Nothing you are saying is making sense, Sean."

"We are friends, Carter. Please, trust me this time. That's what the quakes were and why things were lifting and floating during each quake."

Carter looked at Tabby and back at Sean. "Lifting? Floating?"

"It's true," Holden said. "I saw it too. I didn't say anything because I was afraid no one would believe me. Please, believe my dad, Uncle Carter."

"I saw it in the last fire," Sean said. "I didn't think anyone would believe me either."

"This is insane." Tabitha whispered.

Jenny held up her hands. "It's all true. My father is a scientist. They were on TV around globe warning everyone in the Western Hemisphere to get inside. We are almost out of time. Do it to save the kids, Carter. That is what you and Sean do. Please."

"Okay," Carter said. "But there is nowhere to go. There is no building for miles. You know that."

"What about under the dock?" Holden asked.

Sean stared for a moment, but shook his head. "The water may come up from the lake. We could drown."

Carter cursed and then said, "Sorry. We have rope." He dug three lengths of coiled rope from his pack. "We could tie off to trees."

Rope. That's one of the supplies I should have gotten before leaving the house, Sean thought.

Sean looked at the scrawny trees near the lake. "Too small."

Jenny pointed up the slope. "There are larger ones up there."

Sean gritted his teeth. "Maybe. The roots may still not hold, but we don't have much choice."

"The rocks," Holden said.

"Good idea, buddy," Sean said and smiled. "But they may not be heavy enough either."

"No," Holden said, "Up in those trees is a big outcropping. We could go there."

Sean and Carter met eyes. Sean said, "A cave maybe. Brilliant, Holden. Carter, bring the rope too just in case."

Carter grabbed up the rope and Grant. Sean scooped up Holden and they all ran up the hill.

"Hurry," Jenny said, "we're almost out of time."

They reached the trees and weaved through until they saw the rocks standing tall out of the dirt.

"No cave," Carter said.

Sean put down Holden and grabbed one of the ropes. "We'll tie off here. Kids first."

They backed Holden and Grant up to the rock.

"I'm scared," Grant said.

"Me too. Hurry." Tabby shook her fists. Carter ran around the back of the outcropping and came back. They tied off around the boy's mid sections.

"Too tight," Grant said.

"Sorry, buddy." Carter unraveled the second rope and ran around.

"Okay," Sean said. "Ladies."

He positioned Tabby and Jenny next to and between the boys. Carter and Sean tied them off.

"Hold on to them for good measure," Sean said. Jenny held Holden's hand and Tabitha held Grant.

Carter unraveled the last rope. "You better be right about this or you'll have a lot of explaining to do, brother."

Sean opened his mouth to answer, but he saw pine straw floating up from the ground like backward rain. It was almost beautiful in its terrifyingly surreal way. He thought about the falling grass on the playground. *The dance has started. We're too late.*

Holden whispered. "Dad. The ground."

"I see it." Sean closed his fists in the loops of rope holding his family to the rock. "Carter, we're out of time. Get over here and hold on."

Carter took the end of the rope and ran around the back of the rock. "No, we can make it."

Sean reached his free hand out toward him. "Carter, no, come back now."

Tabitha screamed. "Carter? Sean, help him, please."

All the limbs in the trees rose up as if reaching for the heavens. Flecks of dirt and sand blasted Sean's eyes from the ground along with the backward rain of the pine straw. As Sean blinked, he saw a gray smear of water rising and twisting up above the lake spiraling into the sky. A couple boards from the dock flew up loose into view and then some of the uprooted, smaller trees. A boat shot up through the gray water spire. From the distance, Sean couldn't even tell if it was from the same lake.

His feet picked up off the ground and lifted up into the air behind him. He clinched his fist tighter on the loops and felt his fingers, elbow, and shoulder strain with the upward force. This was more than floating. Sean felt he was being pulled toward the sky by some evil force.

Tabby screamed. "Carter."

Sean saw the loose end of the rope rise past him. He was surprised it wasn't already gone. He made a desperate grab and caught it as the rest of coils whipped out toward the sky. Sean realized he had been standing on it and holding it down until now.

88

The rope pulled taut and strained both of Sean's arms until he cried out in pain.

Jenny was looking upward at the flying debris in the sky. Her hair stood straight up. She breathed. "Oh, no, Carter."

Sean looked up and saw Carter dangling from the end of the rope holding on with both hands a hundred or more feet in the air.

"Carter, climb down here." Sean yelled.

"I can't," Carter said. "It's too strong. I can barely hold on."

Sean saw both their cars twist into the sky in the distance behind Carter's feet – Carter's car and Jenny's jeep. There was going to be trouble when gravity returned to normal. Sean realized he had to get Carter down before normal gravity returned and killed him.

The ground shook and two massive trees tore loose. They flew straight up with their entire root systems. One twisted as it left the ground and just barely missed clipping Carter in the air.

The ground split around other trees as they strained to pull loose.

Carter shouted. "I'm going to let go before I pull us both off, Sean. I'm sorry ... about everything."

"No," Sean said. "Don't let go. Trust me."

"Help him," Tabby said.

Sean rolled his arm around, hooking the rope around his elbow. It wretched his shoulder joint, but he gritted his teeth and rolled his arm again. With each motion, he coiled the rope around his arm pulling Carter down foot by excruciating foot.

"Keep going," Jenny said.

"Great job, Dad!" Holden cheered.

"Hold on, Carter." Tabitha called.

The mass of coil pulled at Sean's weary arm as Carter came within a couple feet of the ground. Sean gave one hard pull and yanked Carter down. He grabbed Carter's wrist, but had no strength left to pull him farther. The rope uncoiled from his arm and snaked up into the sky.

Carter climbed down Sean's body and grabbed the loops of rope himself with one hand. He held around Sean's shoulder with the other. "I owe you one, buddy."

"That was true before the Earth turned upside down," Sean said.

Weight returned and the men dropped to their knees next to the others. Carter and Sean heaved for breath.

"Thank God that's over," Carter said.

Grant said, "Hey, Dad, Carter says he's going to marry Mommy."

"We can talk about that later," Carter said.

One of the cars slammed into the ground a few feet off to their right. Glass shattered and landed all around them. Sean thought, *must not have floated up as high as the rest of the debris.*

A tree slammed onto the rock above them and shattered raining bark down on them.

Then, dirt, water, and pine straw rained down hard and painfully on and around them. It kept piling up.

Grant cried out. "It hurts,

Crater and Sean stood and covered the women and boys with their bodies as best they could. The fallout piled up around their knees and kept rising. The water turned it to mud and made it all heavy. Something large landed with a crash behind them, but Sean couldn't see what it was.

We're going to be buried alive after surviving all of this, he thought.

Michael Strove and Roman Nikitin – Russia

Michael opened his eyes and drew in a long, painful breath full of dust. He rose up dizzy with every bone in his body aching. The station was flattened and they would be dead had they gotten inside.

Roman wasn't moving. Michael shook him and Roman opened his eyes. Michael helped him back up to kneeling.

Roman said, "I don't suppose we can hope that was the last one, can we?"

"Who knows?"

Roman looked back at the flattened forest in the night. "Those tanks won't be bothering us anymore."

Michael looked back. The tanks in the downed forest and the jeeps on the road were a folded mess. He heard people screaming in pain.

"We need to help them," Michael said.

Roman groaned. "Because that is what Brother Carter would do."

"I think so, yes."

"They might shoot you for your trouble, you know."

"You didn't," Michael said.

"I didn't have my gun, but I see your point, Captain Michael." Roman nodded and tottered to his feet. Michael helped him. Roman continued. "The prisons are probably flattened."

Michael led Roman down the hill toward the tanks and the crying voices. He said, "Good point. I'm sure with all this going on, the world has bigger concerns than old, Cold War rivalries."

Roman said, "Yes, maybe, man. Or they might have you rebuild the prison yourself."

"Let's hope for peace and trust." Michael said.

Sean, Carter, and family – Black Fork, Arkansas

Carter used his knife to cut the ropes. Sean dug with his hands. Together they pulled out Tabitha, Jenny, Holden, and Grant. The boys coughed and spit. Grant cried, but everyone was whole.

They climbed up onto the rock and looked out across the land. Most of the trees were uprooted or tilting. The lake was half full of water and debris floated over its surface in a dirty sludge. Smoke from what must have been distant fires rose black into the sky.

Holden pointed. "Dad, Uncle Carter, are you going to put those out?"

"Someone needs to," Sean said.

"Can we ride the truck?" Grant asked and coughed shaking dust and twigs out of his hair.

"Maybe after your dad and I clean up a little, Buddy." Carter jumped down and walked across the debris field. He swept straw and dirt away from the back of the car on its side until he could read the plate. Carter groaned. "I almost had it paid off too. No chance you are parked close by, is there, Sean?"

Sean shrugged. "I saw Jenny's jeep go up in the air with yours. I'm not sure where it landed."

"Maybe we should keep an eye on the sky," Holden said.

Sean rubbed his hand over Holden's head. Dust sprinkled out of it and Holden sneezed. Sean knelt down and hugged both boys. Jenny put her arm around Sean's shoulder. Tabitha jumped down and fell into Carter's arms. No one said anything for a while.

"What now?" Jenny asked.

Carter said, "We need to hike out. Find people."

"You think anyone else survived?" Tabitha asked.

"People made it," Sean said. "A lot of them need help, but that's what we do, right?"

Holden took his father's hand. "All of us. That's what we all do."

Carter looked at the sun and then pointed. "This is east and the direction of home. Let's see what we can find."

They all walked out of the wilderness together.

***

About the author:

John Freitas is an author of speculative fiction that lives in Southeast Texas. He has a background in electronics and computer science.

Other works:

The Quantum Brain
Oh Hell No!
The Quantum Brain Maximum Speed

On the web scifibookseries.com

Made in the USA
Charleston, SC
01 June 2016